BAD COMPANY

Jill walked back to the dorm with Bridget.

"How do you like it at the International Ice Academy so far?" Bridget asked her.

"It's pretty tough," Jill replied. "But I'm slowly getting the hang of things and getting to know people. Kevin seems like a really nice guy."

When Bridget didn't answer right away, Jill added, "And he's really cute too—don't you think?"

"Jill," Bridget said, "I wouldn't get too close to Kevin if I were you."

Jill stopped short. "Why not?"

Bridget lowered her voice. "You mean, you really don't know?" she said. "You haven't heard the dirt on Kevin?"

Silver Blades

titles in Large-Print Editions:

GOING
FOR THE GOLD

Melissa Lowell

Created by Parachute Press

Gareth Stevens Publishing
MILWAUKEE

For a free color catalog describing Gareth Stevens' list of high-quality books and multimedia programs, call 1-800-542-2595 (USA) or 1-800-461-9120 (Canada). Gareth Stevens Publishing's Fax: (414) 225-0377. See our catalog, too, on the World Wide Web: http://gsinc.com

Library of Congress Cataloging-in-Publication Data

Lowell, Melissa.
    Going for the gold / Melissa Lowell.
      p. cm. — (Silver blades; #4)
    Summary: When Jill Wong is invited to train at one of the best ice skating schools in the country, her adjustment to the new situation is harder than she expected.
    ISBN 0-8368-2066-5 (lib. bdg.)
    [1. Ice skating—Fiction. 2. Chinese Americans—Fiction.]
  I. Title. II. Series: Lowell, Melissa. Silver blades; #4.
PZ7.L96456Go 1998
[Fic]—dc21   97-39607

First published in this edition in 1998 by
Gareth Stevens Publishing
1555 North RiverCenter Drive, Suite 201
Milwaukee, WI 53212 USA

Printed in the United States of America

1 2 3 4 5 6 7 8 9 02 01 00 99 98

"**W**hat about 'Hip-Hop on Ice'?" Jill Wong said as she sat down to untie her skates. Her long black braid, tied with a red ribbon, fell over her shoulder.

"Hey, that's not bad," said Danielle Panati. She pulled the purple headband from her thick, honey-brown hair. "We could draw a picture of a rabbit on the poster—a rabbit on skates. Get it?"

Jill laughed, but Tori Carsen rolled her blue eyes and said, "Very funny, you guys. 'Hip-Hop on Ice.' I can really see Mr. Weiler going for that."

Franz Weiler was the director of and coach for Silver Blades, the girls' figure-skating club. He was a short, balding man with a slight German accent. "Mr. Weiler's probably never even *heard* of hip-hop," Jill said. "Anyway, I was only kidding."

"It's better than nothing," Nikki Simon said. She was slim and green-eyed with wavy brown hair, freckles, and braces on her teeth. "We've got to come up with *something* for the ice show. This is my first spring show with Silver Blades, so it has to be fantastic. You guys told me that the kids in the club always think of the theme for the spring show. And we can't plan a fund-raiser until we think of a theme."

"And we can't raise any money until we hold a fund-raiser," said Tori.

"And we can't have the show at all if we can't raise the money," said Danielle.

It was a Friday afternoon at the end of February, and Jill, Danielle, Tori, and Nikki had just finished their second skating practice of the day. All four girls were seventh-graders, serious figure skaters, and best friends. Jill loved hanging out with her friends after Friday practices, laughing and joking. They worked so hard all week, it was nice to relax a little.

But Jill didn't mind the hard work either. Silver Blades was one of the best figure-skating clubs in the country, and Jill's skating had improved enormously there. She had just won her first big competition, the northeastern junior Regionals, in Lake Placid, New York. And then she had placed sixth in the eastern junior Sectionals, where she competed against the best skaters on the entire East Coast. The next step was national competition. Jill's coach, Kathy Bart, had high hopes for her. Jill had high hopes for herself too. More than anything she wanted to be a skating champion.

Tori broke into Jill's thoughts. "You've got to come

up with something, Jill," she said in her slightly bossy way. "You're supposed to be the creative one." Tori was petite, with curly blond hair. She was changing into jeans and a pair of brand-new running shoes. She seemed to have a new pair of shoes every week.

"I'll think about it over the weekend," said Jill. She frowned, rubbing a fresh blister on her heel. "Does anybody have a bandage?"

"Kathy's got some in her office," said Danielle. "But the door is closed."

"Still?" said Tori. "She's been in there for an hour."

"That's weird," said Jill. "She never closes her door. I wonder what's going on."

Still in her bare feet, Jill tiptoed out of the girls' locker room. Tori, Nikki, and Danielle followed her.

Kathy's door *was* closed. "Do you think I should knock?" Jill whispered.

Tori shook her head and put her finger to her lips. "Listen."

Jill stood perfectly still and listened. There were voices coming from Kathy's office: Kathy's strong, no-nonsense voice, and two others, a man's and a woman's. Jill didn't recognize the other voices. They both had slight foreign accents.

"We would like to see her skate again," the woman was saying.

"Yes," said the man. "We were very impressed with her at the Regionals. We think she can go far—very far."

"I'm sure that can be arranged," said Kathy.

All four girls stared at one another, wide-eyed. "Who are they talking about?" Tori whispered.

Jill shrugged.

"Excuse me for a moment," Kathy said. They heard her chair scrape the floor.

"She's coming!" said Nikki.

The girls hurried back to the locker room before Kathy could catch them. Peeking from behind the locker-room door, they saw Kathy step out of her office and into Mr. Weiler's. In a few seconds she was back, carrying a piece of paper. She shut her office door behind her.

"What was *that* all about?" said Danielle.

"I don't know," said Jill. "I sure wish there was a way to find out."

"Jill, it's about time we did some serious work on your double axel," Kathy Bart said. "I know you can nail your current program. It's never too early to start working on the next one."

Jill nodded and skated over to her coach, who was standing in the center of the rink. It was Saturday afternoon, and Jill was having her private lesson with Kathy. Eight other kids were on the ice as well, practicing in small groups.

Jill hadn't forgotten about the mysterious strangers in Kathy's office the day before. She was dying to know who they were.

But I'll never get up the nerve to ask, she thought, glancing at Kathy, who was dressed in sweats, a blue down vest, and a wool cap, her dark-blond hair pulled back in a ponytail. Kathy was a serious young woman in her late twenties, and a tough, demanding coach whose nickname was "Sarge." Jill and Kathy could talk about skating for hours, but Kathy was a very private person, and Jill knew she didn't appreciate snooping.

"I know you can get enough height on your jump," Kathy went on. "It's a matter of getting used to completing the revolutions quickly enough. The double axel is often harder than many triple jumps, because you take off from the edge of your blade and not with your toepick."

Jill nodded, tugging at the sleeve of her plain red skating dress. Red was Jill's favorite color, and she wore it almost every day.

"Remember when we went from singles to doubles with other jumps?" asked Kathy.

Jill nodded. "I think I still have the bruises."

"Well, get ready for some more," Kathy said. "So show me what you can do. Start off with a few single axels, then when you're ready, go for a double."

Jill started to circle the outside of the rink with backward crossovers, building speed. A single axel required one and a half rotations in the air—a sort of a waltz jump and a loop jump combined into one. When she was ready, Jill stepped into a forward outside edge. As she lifted her body off the ice, she pulled in her arms, rotated one and a half times, keeping her left leg crossed over her right. She landed solidly on her right skate and opened her arms for balance, extending her left leg behind her.

"Good!" Kathy called to her.

Jill decided to go right for the double axel. She'd never landed it before. But if she thought about it too much, she knew she'd lose her nerve.

This time she concentrated on building up more speed before the takeoff. She quickly lifted into the air. One . . . two and a half times she turned—and a split second later she found herself sitting on the ice.

"You didn't get enough height," Kathy said.

"No kidding," Jill muttered. She got up and brushed the snow from her wool tights.

Jill spent the next hour trying to land a double axel, but she fell every time.

"It's coming along," Kathy said, calling an end to their practice. "But you really need to concentrate. In fact you need to get all your double and triple jumps up to par if you're going to have a shot at the senior ladies' division next year."

"Senior ladies'—next year?" Jill repeated. Even though she'd been hoping for the same thing herself, she hadn't realized Kathy thought it was a serious possibility.

"Yes, I talked to some of the judges at the Sectionals," Kathy said. "They said they think you have a definite shot at it."

"Are you serious?" Jill asked.

"Jill, I'm very serious." Kathy adjusted her wool cap. "The level of your skating isn't quite high enough yet, but in another six to nine months I think you could be ready. Of course—"

"It's going to take a lot of hard work," Jill finished the sentence for her. She nodded. "As always."

Kathy shook her head. "Not as always—even more than that."

"I'm ready to work hard, as hard as I can," Jill vowed. "I mean it. I want to make it to senior Nationals more than anything."

"I know," Kathy said. "You wouldn't have made it this far if you didn't." She smiled at Jill and added, "See you Monday."

Jill pulled her light-blue Silver Blades warm-up jacket over her shoulders and skated around the rink a few times before getting off the ice. Ever since she won the regional competition in Lake Placid, she'd felt as though her skating career was moving in fast-forward. Now Kathy was actually talking about her going to the senior ladies' Nationals, and Jill was only thirteen.

It's all up to me, she reminded herself. If I want to do it, I can. And Kathy's going to help me, every step of the way.

As she stepped off the ice, Jill suddenly noticed two vaguely familiar faces in the arena. A small woman with a long nose, a strong chin, straight, dark eyebrows, and very short brown hair was sitting in the stands watching the practice. With her was a tall, pale man with red hair.

Tori was standing just off the ice. She'd obviously noticed the woman too.

"Do you know who that is?" she whispered to Jill.

Jill shook her head. "They look familiar," she said, "but I can't place them."

"I think it's Ludmila Petrova," said Tori. "You know, the famous Russian coach? She trained all those Olympic skaters back in the eighties. And *he* looks like Simon Wells, the ice dancer!"

Jill nodded. "Of course," she said. Over the past few years she'd spent hours watching tapes of Ludmila Petrova and Simon Wells, both video recordings of their Olympic performances as well as some coaching tapes they had made. And when Jill and some of the others in Silver Blades recently competed in the Regionals, they'd heard rumors that the two famous skaters were in the audience. "I wonder if they were the people in Kathy's office yesterday?" she asked now.

"I don't know." Tori shrugged. "But we'll find out soon. They're coming down here."

Jill watched as the man and woman approached Kathy, who'd been chatting at rinkside with Paul Delaney, another member of Silver Blades.

The coaches spoke for a few minutes.

Tori looked at Jill. "What do you think they're doing here?"

"I don't know," said Jill, slipping her skate guards

over her blades. "Maybe they're just passing through town."

Tori laughed. "Since when does anybody just pass through Seneca Hills?"

"You have a point," Jill said with a giggle. "Anyway, let's go get changed."

The girls were halfway up the bleachers when Kathy called, "Jill, could you hold up a second?"

Jill turned around and saw Kathy and the two famous figure skaters looking at her. "Sure." She glanced back at Tori, who raised her eyebrows. "I'll see you in the locker room," Jill said. Tori turned reluctantly and left.

"Jill, I'd like to introduce you to two of the most important people in the world of ice-skating," Kathy said in a serious tone. "Jill Wong, this is Ludmila Petrova." Ludmila held out her hand, and Jill shook it. "And this is Simon Wells." Jill shook his hand too.

"Hi," Jill said. "It's really nice to meet you."

"The pleasure is all ours," Simon said with a British accent. Jill immediately recognized it. So these *were* the people she'd overheard in Kathy's office! "Jill, we enjoyed watching you practice this afternoon."

"We also saw you compete at the junior Regionals in Lake Placid," Ludmila said. She smiled briefly. "Very nice. Very smooth."

"Thank you." Jill blushed. She wasn't usually embarrassed by praise, but she wasn't used to hearing it from people she admired so much.

"We have come to talk to you about something," Ludmila went on. "Have you heard about our training facility?"

"The International Ice Academy?" said Jill. "In Denver?"

Simon nodded.

Jill had heard of it, all right. Every skater in the country wanted to go to the International Ice Academy. They had the best of everything: the best coaches, the best facilities, the best skaters. Only a few of the most promising young skaters in the world were chosen to train there.

"So you're familiar with our school," said Ludmila. "Good. Now I have another question for you. How would you like to go there?"

Jill thought her heart would stop beating on the spot. *Me?!* she thought in amazement. Is Ludmila Petrova really asking *me* to go to the Academy?

"I—I'd love to," she stammered.

Ludmila smiled. "I'm glad to hear it, Jill. We want very much for you to come and train with us."

"In fact," Simon added, "we'd like you to come as soon as possible."

Jill still couldn't believe it. Her face must have shown her astonishment, because both Simon and Ludmila nodded and laughed.

"Isn't this fantastic news?" Kathy said. "I've been dying to tell you all day, Jill, but I didn't want to make you nervous. It's not that I want to get rid of you, of course, but this is an unbelievable opportunity."

Jill just swallowed and nodded. She was so shocked, she could hardly speak. Ludmila Petrova wanted to train her!

"Kathy has called your parents, and they've invited us to meet with them tonight," Ludmila said, pulling her coat tighter around her. "We'll come to your house after dinner and explain everything then."

"That's great!" Jill said. But inside she was wondering how her parents would react to the news. The Academy was probably very expensive—and Jill had six younger brothers and sisters. Her parents didn't have much money to spare. And she wasn't sure how they'd feel about letting her live so far away.

Ludmila nodded. "Good. We'll see you tonight, then."

Jill walked to the locker room like a zombie. Ludmila Petrova had trained the last three national champions—and her eye for talent was famous. Being chosen by her was something every serious skater dreamed of. And now it had happened to Jill!

She paused and sat down for a second. Her head was spinning.

It's amazing, she thought. It's like my whole life has changed in one instant. Yesterday I was helping my friends plan the spring ice show. Now I could be moving to Denver!

"**J**ill would be skating almost six hours a day," Ludmila Petrova explained to Mr. and Mrs. Wong. Jill was sitting between her mother and father on the living-room sofa, opposite Ludmila and Simon Wells. She listened anxiously as Ludmila explained the Academy's program to her parents.

"We have several coaches who concentrate on the junior level, most of them from Europe. We offer intensive dance training as well."

"What about school?" asked Jill's father. "When is there time for that?"

"Every morning the students receive private and group tutoring from certified teachers on the premises," Simon told him. "They get at least four hours of study each day."

Mrs. Wong poured some more tea into Jill's cup and handed it to her. Jill took a sip, nervously looking from her father, to Simon, to her mother, to Ludmila, and then back to her father again. So far neither of her parents seemed very excited about the idea of Jill's training at the Academy.

"All of our pupils are expected to keep up with their grades," Ludmila went on. "Skating comes first, of course, but we don't neglect their education."

"And where would Jill live? In some sort of dormitory?" Jill's mother looked concerned.

"We try to be a home away from home. We have two very large Victorian-style houses with nice rooms for the students. Each house has a full staff living in to look after the students, and our chef provides nutritionally balanced meals," Ludmila said.

Simon nodded. "We even have a TV in each dorm lobby," he whispered to Jill.

Everyone laughed.

"It doesn't sound like you'll have much time to watch it," Mr. Wong commented with a wry smile.

Jill nodded. "I won't miss it. Would I have a roommate?" she asked.

"Yes, everyone shares a room," Ludmila said. "It keeps you from getting lonely—and it's also less expensive that way."

Uh-oh, Jill thought. Here it comes. They were going to start talking about money. That would probably put an end to any further discussion of her attending the International Ice Academy.

Mr. Wong cleared his throat. "We do need to have some idea of the cost," he said.

Ludmila handed him a brochure and a couple of sheets of paper. "This will give you a basic idea. Simon and I can get you an exact listing of Jill's expenses tomorrow if you like."

Jill stared at her father. His eyes seemed to be widening in disbelief as he read through the brochure and studied the papers. "Well, the rink looks beautiful. Jill, did you see this picture?" he asked as he held up the photo of a gleaming Olympic-size rink.

Jill nodded. She was waiting for her father to say something about the cost, one way or the other, but instead he seemed absorbed in reading the papers. Well, he hasn't said it's impossible, Jill consoled herself.

"We should mention that there is a general scholarship fund," Simon added. "We've brought an application. If you are awarded financial aid, it might not cover all of the costs, but it would certainly help."

Mr. Wong nodded. "Good."

"So what do you think?" Simon asked, smiling at the Wongs. "How does this all sound?"

"It sounds excellent," Jill chimed in quickly. Then she looked uncertainly at her parents.

"It does sound wonderful for Jill," her mother said. "But we'd like a few days to think it over. Is that all right?"

"Of course." Simon tapped an extra brochure against his leg. "Would the end of the week be too soon? I'll make sure you hear about the scholarship before then."

Mrs. Wong looked at Jill. "That should be fine," she said.

"You must understand—we don't want to rush you. It's only that we're anxious to start," Ludmila explained. "We don't usually recruit students in the middle of the school year. But one of our students had to leave, so we are fortunate enough to have this opening now for you, Jill."

Jill smiled nervously. "We'll definitely let you know by next weekend."

"Fine. Just call us when you're ready," Ludmila said, rising to leave. She handed Jill a business card with her name on it. "We're going back to Colorado tonight, but if you have any questions, feel free to call anytime."

Jill nodded.

"Thank you so much for coming over," said Mrs. Wong.

"We'll look forward to hearing from you," Simon said, and everyone said their good-byes.

The second Ludmila and Simon left the house, Jill turned to her parents. "Well? What do you think?" she asked eagerly.

"I think it sounds fantastic," Mrs. Wong said. "I wish *I* could go."

"It looks beautiful," Mr. Wong agreed. "And it's a great opportunity. But how would you feel about moving so far away?"

"Well, I'd miss everybody like crazy," Jill said. "But I think it would be the best thing for my skating."

"Definitely," Mr. Wong agreed. "These people have what it takes to make skaters into champions, that's for sure." He glanced at the list of current and former skaters from the Academy. "Pretty impressive. Jill, you should be proud of yourself. This is a big honor."

"I am," Jill said. "But . . . well, you guys haven't said anything about the money yet. Is it really expensive?"

Mrs. Wong cleared her throat. "Let's not talk about that yet. I think you should make your decision based on whether it's the right thing to do, for you and for your skating, right now. If it is, then we'll work out the money somehow."

It *is* the right thing for me to do, Jill thought to herself. I just know it is!

"Dani, you're not going to believe this," Jill said when Danielle answered the phone later that evening.

"Tori told me," Danielle said. "Ludmila Petrova and Simon Wells wanted to talk to you! What happened? What did they say?"

"It's so cool," Jill said. "They really want me to come to the Ice Academy and train with them!"

"Well, of course they do. Did you think they came two thousand miles just to look at the scenery?" Danielle joked.

Jill laughed.

"So when do they want you to go?" Danielle asked.

"As soon as possible," Jill said. "But my parents are still deciding about it. It makes me really nervous, just thinking about going and skating with all those kids from around the world. You should see the rink, Dani. It's gorgeous. And they have—"

"Jill, this is so great—but it's also so *terrible*," said Danielle, abruptly interrupting her.

"What do you mean?" Jill asked.

"You'll be moving to Denver," Danielle said. "We've been best friends since elementary school. Between skating and school, I feel as if I've seen you almost every day of my life. Everything's going to be so boring without you—school, Silver Blades, weekends. . . ."

"I know, Dani," Jill said softly. "I'm trying not to think about that part of it. At least you'll still have Nikki and Tori. Think about how much I'm going to miss you guys. I won't know anyone out there." Jill traced a mark on the pantry wall where her brother Henry had recently been measured. There were tiny pencil marks all up and down the wall, with marks for all of them. She couldn't imagine living apart from her family either.

"You'll know everyone in about ten seconds, Jill," Danielle said. "Since when have you ever had a hard time meeting people?"

"Still, it won't be the same," Jill insisted. "I'll never find friends like you and Nikki and Tori. Especially *you*, Danielle." Just then Jill felt a tug on the telephone cord. Her little brother Michael was looking up at her.

"You promised to read me a story before I go to bed," he said.

"All right, Mikey. I'll be right there," Jill said. "Dani, I've got to go read a bedtime story to Michael. Who knows—if I go to the Academy, I might actually have *more* free time than I do at home!"

Danielle laughed. "I'll talk to you tomorrow. Let me know the minute your parents decide."

"I will," said Jill.

Jill hung up the phone and walked upstairs to her brother's bedroom. She picked out one of her favorite storybooks from his shelf and sat on the side of his bed, waiting for Michael to say good night to her parents. All she could think about was going to Colorado.

Jill peeled a carrot and started slicing it. She was standing at the kitchen counter helping her parents with dinner. It was Friday night, and she couldn't stand the suspense any longer. Ever since Ludmila and Simon's visit, her parents had barely said anything, one way or the other, about her going to the Academy. They seemed very busy gathering information, filling out forms, and talking to the Academy's financial-aid office.

"Um, Mom and Dad?" she began. "Have you been thinking any more about—you know—the Academy?"

Mrs. Wong laughed. "I've been thinking about it constantly," she said, turning to her husband. "What about you, dear?"

"Nonstop," said Mr. Wong. "I don't suppose *you've* given it any thought, have you, Jill?" he joked.

"I can't think about anything else," Jill said. "It's driving me crazy." She paused and looked at both her parents. "I really want to go."

Mr. Wong looked serious. "Well, Jill, we *have* made a decision," he said.

Jill looked at him nervously and held her breath.

"Ludmila called today about our financial-aid application."

"And—?" said Jill. She toyed with a button on her red sweater. The frown on her father's face was a bad sign.

But then he broke into a broad grin. "And—it was approved!" he exclaimed. "They're giving you a scholarship!"

"You mean—I can go?"

Both of her parents nodded.

"Oh, thank you!" Jill squealed. She tossed the vegetable peeler into the air and ran to give them both big hugs. "Mom and Dad, you're the greatest!"

They hugged her back, hard. Mrs. Wong had tears in her eyes.

"We had decided to let you go no matter what," she said. "But the financial aid certainly helps."

"After dinner we'll call the Academy and tell Ludmila and Simon you're coming for sure," said Mr. Wong.

"I can't believe it!" Jill said, her heart fluttering with excitement. "I'm going to the International Ice Academy!"

3

"**S**urprise!"

The lights in the weight room flashed on, and Jill took a step backward, startled. All the members of Silver Blades were crowded into the small room. Tori, Danielle, and Nikki were standing up in front, beaming at her. A banner that said GOOD-BYE AND GOOD LUCK! hung on the wall behind everyone, and a large cake in the shape of a skate was on a table near the door. Red and white balloons dangled from the ceiling.

"You guys!" Jill blinked, feeling a huge lump growing in her throat. "I don't believe this!"

The weight trainer, Ernie Harper, stepped out from behind the door and put his arm around her. "And you thought you were going to a weight-training session. Do you think I'd let you spend your last session with me lifting weights?"

Everyone laughed and clapped. Nikki, Tori, and Danielle ran to Jill and hugged her. It was Saturday afternoon, two weeks after Jill's decision, and today was Jill's last day at the Seneca Hills Ice Arena.

Mr. Weiler stepped forward to shake Jill's hand. "Congratulations, Jill, and good luck," he said. "We're really going to miss you around here."

"Thanks," Jill said. "I'll miss you too." She saw Kathy smiling warmly at her and added, "You, too, Sarge."

"Cut the cake already!" a tall ninth-grader named Bobby Rodgers called out, and everyone started laughing.

"Okay, okay!" Jill said. "Just give me a second." She picked up a knife and started cutting the cake into squares.

"Two, please." Alex Beekman, who was Nikki's pairs partner, held out a plate.

Jill served him two large pieces.

"Hey, I hope you have fun out there. I'd give anything to go to Denver," Alex said. "Send us postcards, okay?"

Jill nodded and served the next piece to Hillary Ford, a third-grader. "There you go."

"Jill, you're so lucky," Hillary said, her blue eyes shining with admiration. "Will you come back and visit?"

"Definitely," Jill told her. "Silver Blades is my home away from home. I'll be back every chance I get."

Jill held out a plate of cake to Diana Mitchell. Sixteen years old, with dramatic looks and fiery-red hair,

Diana had been considered the best skater in Silver Blades for as long as Jill could remember. Jill still couldn't get over the fact that Ludmila had picked her and not Diana. She wondered if Diana was upset about it.

"Are you excited?" Diana asked, picking up a fork from the table.

Jill nodded. "But nervous, mostly."

"Don't be," Diana said. "I'm sure you'll do great." She smiled.

"Thanks," Jill said. Diana genuinely seemed to wish her well. "I hope so."

"Who knows? Maybe we'll be competing against each other at senior Nationals someday."

"It would be amazing to skate with you," Jill said. "You're so good."

"Well, Ludmila Petrova seems to think you're pretty great too," Diana replied. She gave Jill a hug and another warm smile and walked across the weight room to talk with Melinda Daly.

One by one the members of Silver Blades came up to Jill to get a piece of cake and wish her well. Jill realized how many good friends she had made at the rink. She couldn't imagine not skating with them every morning at dawn and then again in the afternoons. She tried to tell everyone how much she'd miss them.

The last people in line were Tori, Danielle, and Nikki. "Stop cutting the cake," Tori commanded, "or you'll never get the chance to eat some yourself." She took the cake knife from Jill's hand, set it down beside the cake, and handed her a plate. Jill picked up a fork and dug in.

"So were you surprised?" Danielle asked.

"Way surprised," Jill said. "How did you guys keep this a secret? We've been hanging out together all week, and I didn't have a clue."

"I guess you're just a little on the slow side," Nikki teased her. "Actually it was almost impossible. I kept almost asking you to *help* us plan it, because you're usually the one who plans parties around here."

"I still can't believe you're really going," Tori said. "When my mother found out, she had a fit."

Tori's mother was determined to see Tori succeed as a figure skater. She wanted Tori to have every advantage and put lots of pressure on her to win. In fact Mrs. Carsen attended almost every Silver Blades practice and constantly criticized Tori's performance.

"My mom said she didn't understand why we *both* couldn't study with Ludmila Petrova," Tori added.

Jill gave her friend a hug. She knew Tori wanted to go to the Academy more than anything but was trying not to let it show. Several times in the past Tori's jealousy of Jill had caused arguments between them. Jill had tried to help Tori stand up for herself around her mom. And lately, Jill was happy to see, it seemed that Tori was doing this and was much happier.

Mr. Weiler clapped his hands together. "Attention, everyone! Believe it or not, we will still have practice today, in about half an hour. But before then

I'm going to make the official presentation of Jill's send-off present."

Then Mr. Weiler handed Jill a large box wrapped in blue paper with white ribbon around it. "Every member chipped in. We hope you like it."

Jill tore off the paper and opened the box. "It's red—I'm shocked!" she said, laughing. She pulled out a thick, hooded sweatshirt that said SILVER BLADES on the front and SENECA HILLS, PENNSYLVANIA, on the back. "But the club's colors are light blue and white," Jill said.

"I know, but we know you love red," Kathy said. "And we thought you might wear the sweatshirt more often this way."

"I love it. Thanks, everyone!" Jill held the sweatshirt up against her body. It was extra large, just the way she liked to wear them.

"Speech! Speech!" Mitchell Bowen yelled.

"Yeah, you have to give a speech before you can go!" Sara Russell added.

"They're right," Mr. Weiler agreed. "It's a tradition."

"Well . . . okay. But you know I'm not good at sentimental speeches. Just give me a second." Jill went over to the stereo and popped one of her favorite hip-hop tapes into the tape deck. "I'd just like to say . . . thanks a lot, everybody. I'm going to miss you guys a ton. And . . . start dancing!" She pressed the play button, and dance music boomed out into the weight room.

"Hey, Jill!" Tori called over the music. "Hip-hop on

ice!" Tori wrinkled up her nose, held her hands in front of her as if they were paws, and started doing the bunny hop. She gave her hips an extra wiggle to make it look funny.

Jill put her hands on Tori's waist and hopped behind her. Next Nikki joined in, then Danielle. Soon everybody was doing the bunny hop in one long line that snaked through the weight room and out the door. Even Mr. Weiler joined in, hopping and laughing so hard, he almost forgot all about practice.

I'm really going to miss Silver Blades, Jill thought as the party was winding down. Will I be able to find such good friends at the Academy? she wondered. Am I really doing the right thing?

"**Y**ou can't forget this." Mrs. Wong handed Jill a framed photograph of the entire family that Jill kept on top of her dresser.

Jill tucked it into her suitcase, in between some heavy wool sweaters. It was Sunday night, and she was leaving for Denver the next morning.

"You're definitely going to need this." Henry, Jill's ten-year-old brother, started rolling up her poster of Katarina Witt, the 1984 and 1988 Olympic gold medalist.

"I can't believe I get my own room now," Kristi said. She was eight and Randi was six, and they'd been sharing a room since Randi was born. Now Randi was going to have to share her room with Laurie, who was only one year old and who used to sleep in their parents' room. "I can't wait to move in," Kristi went on. She stood in the doorway, holding some of her games and stuffed animals.

"It looks like you've moved in already," Jill teased as Kristi put some things on the floor. "Just remember, it's not permanent. I do plan to come home to visit very soon. And who knows how things will turn out. . . ."

"Then *you* can share a room with Randi and Laurie," Kristi said.

"No fair!" Randi cried. They started playing tug-of-war with one of Kristi's stuffed animals.

"What do you mean, you don't know how things will turn out?" Mrs. Wong asked Jill, a concerned expression on her face.

"Well . . . it's just that I'm nervous, Mom," Jill said softly. "I don't plan on coming back. I mean, not right away anyway, but maybe I won't be good enough."

Mrs. Wong shook her head firmly. "The coaches wouldn't have chosen you if you weren't good enough. Trust me—you won't be needing this room anymore, honey."

Jill grinned. "You sound like you can't wait to get rid of me!" Her mother laughed and folded up one of Jill's skating dresses. "It's not that, and you know it. I just want you to feel ready to leave, that's all."

Tears sprung into Jill's eyes. Quickly she brushed them away. "I am ready," she said, her voice shaky. "I still want to go more than anything. It's just going to be so weird, living in a dorm and everything. . . ."

"Well, just remember, there are a lot of other girls

in the same situation as you," Mrs. Wong said. "You'll all be far from home, without your families. You'll probably make some very close friends."

Jill nodded and stuffed another pair of socks into the suitcase.

"And we'll always be here for you if you ever want to call and talk."

Jill sniffed. If Mom keeps going on like this, she thought, I'll start crying for sure.

Her mother seemed to read her mind. "And think of how much you'll learn, Jill," she said. "Ludmila is offering you a chance to become a champion—and you're taking it. You're doing the right thing, Jill. I feel sure of it. Your father and I are behind you one hundred percent."

"Thanks, Mom." Jill kissed her mother on the cheek. As long as she focused on skating, she could bear a little homesickness.

"I brought you a survival kit," Mr. Wong said, walking into the room. He handed Jill a cookie tin. "These should last you at least to the airport."

Jill took off the lid and sniffed the delicious chocolate chip cookies her father had made. "These are great, Dad. I'll definitely miss your cookies."

"Quick—hide them, or your sisters will eat them all," Mr. Wong advised, and Jill tucked them into her carry-on bag.

"Okay, Jill—you'd better get some sleep," Mrs. Wong said. "You have a long trip tomorrow. Come on, girls, Henry." Jill's twin brothers, Michael and Mark, and her youngest sister, Laurie, were already in bed. Jill smiled as she hugged Randi and Kristi good night.

"Wait a second. I have something I want to give you." Randi broke away from the hug and ran out of the room. She returned a minute later, holding her favorite, ratty old teddy bear. She handed it to Jill, and a little stuffing fell out onto the floor.

"Are you sure you want to give me Mr. Grizzly?" Jill asked, running her fingers over the frayed ears of the stuffed bear.

"Yes," Randi said. "You might need him. In case you get lonely."

Jill smiled at her sister and hugged the bear close. She needed him already.

"Seat thirteen-C, Miss Wong. We'll be boarding in a few minutes."

"Thanks." Jill tucked her boarding pass into her jacket pocket, gave her parents a final hug and kiss, and went over to her three best friends, who were waiting by the gate to say good-bye. "Well, I guess this is it," Jill said.

"I really don't want to say good-bye," Danielle said. "You're going to be so far away. We're talking thousands and thousands of miles away."

"Actually it's only fifteen hundred and eighty-seven miles," Nikki corrected her. "I checked on my dad's road atlas."

"Like that matters," Tori said. "It's not as if we'll get to drive out there."

"Not until we turn sixteen anyway," Nikki reminded her. "Then we can get our licenses and come visit."

"In the meantime we made this for you." Danielle took a three-ring notebook out of her shoulder bag and handed it to Jill. "So you won't forget us when you're famous." She tried to smile, but a tear ran down her cheek.

"Thanks." Jill opened the notebook. Inside there were pictures of all of them, and of other skaters from Silver Blades, with quotes pasted on top of the photos. There were old programs from Silver Blades shows, a tiny picture of Jill that had appeared in *Skating* magazine the month before, and even a menu from Vinni's, their favorite pizza place. "This is so great. I love this!"

"Jill, I'm so jealous. You're going to get so good!" Tori said.

"The club's going to be so boring without you," Danielle said.

"Yeah, who's going to make fun of everyone?" asked Nikki.

"Who's going to wear red?" Tori added.

Jill laughed. "Maybe one of you guys could take over."

Just then the flight attendants began boarding the passengers, and Jill knew it was time to say goodbye.

She looked at Nikki. "Well . . . good luck," Nikki said, then gave Jill a big hug. "Make sure you write us lots of letters."

"You guys have to write back," Jill said, hugging Tori next. "I want to know all the dirt on everybody."

"We will," Tori promised.

Jill turned to hug Danielle and stopped. She could see the tears in her friend's big brown eyes. Saying good-bye to her friends, especially Danielle, was as hard as leaving her family.

"I'm really going to miss you," Jill said, trying not to cry as she gave Danielle a big hug.

"Take care," Danielle managed to say as the tears slowly trickled down her cheek.

Jill bit her lip, picked up her bags, and walked over to the flight attendant at the door. Then she turned around and waved at them again. "Don't let Mr. Weiler and Kathy work you too hard!" she called.

"Are you crazy?" Tori replied. "We're already taking today off, in honor of you."

Jill smiled and turned to walk down onto the plane. She had never felt so happy and so sad at the same time. She felt as if she were closing a door on her old life—and stepping into a whole new world.

5

Jill glanced out the window at the Rocky Mountains as the plane started to make its final descent into Denver. She'd be at the International Ice Academy in less than an hour. She had never been away from home on her own before, but she wasn't scared really, just a little nervous, and very excited about meeting skaters from all over the country—and the world.

She'd never lived anywhere but plain old Seneca Hills. It was a nice enough town, but it could get a little boring, she thought, examining Denver's skyline and the snow-capped mountain peaks. The bright sunlight reflected off the tall office buildings and skyscrapers downtown, and Jill felt a swarm of butterflies in her stomach. *This is it. I'm here.*

The plane touched down, and several minutes later Jill walked down the aisle, off the plane, and into the terminal. She glanced around, looking for Ludmila or Simon. She didn't see them anywhere.

I hope they haven't forgotten about me, Jill thought anxiously. The butterflies in her stomach got worse. What will I do if they're not here?

Then she saw a man holding up a sign with big black lettering: JILL WONG. Relieved, she walked over to him, smiling nervously. "Hi. I'm Jill Wong."

"I'm from the Ice Academy. Come this way." He turned abruptly and led her out of the gate area to the ground floor, where a limousine was waiting.

"But—what about my luggage?" Jill asked, following him.

"They'll send it over later." He opened the door with a flourish, and Jill slid into the plush interior of the limo. "Help yourself to some soda water or juice." He pointed out the small refrigerator in the back seat. "The Academy's about forty-five minutes from here."

No wonder this place is so expensive, Jill thought, twisting off the top of a bottle of cranberry juice as the driver pulled the limo out into traffic. I can't wait to tell everyone how I was treated like royalty!

"Jill, welcome to the International Ice Academy! I'm Lisa Welch, your dorm parent. I coach part-time at the rink too. I work with the younger kids, so you probably won't see me much there."

"It's nice to meet you." Jill shook Lisa's hand. Lisa was about thirty-five years old, with short brown hair, warm brown eyes, and a round face. Dressed in jeans and a sweater, she was of average height, with a skater's strong-looking legs.

Jill looked around the lobby of the dorm, which was called the Aspen House. It was a very large, old house, with a piano in the living room, comfortable-looking couches and chairs, and a television and VCR.

"Ludmila's coaching right now, so she asked me to show you around. Come on upstairs and we'll take a look at your room." Lisa led her to the stairs, pointing out her own apartment on the way. "This is where I live. You can come see me anytime, about anything."

Jill's room was on the second floor, on a hall with five other large rooms. When Lisa opened the door, Jill gasped. She couldn't believe what a beautiful view she had from her window: it looked straight out on the mountains, which were covered with snow.

"This is great," Jill said as she set her small carry-on bag down on the floor. The room was very spacious, and the furniture was simple but new-looking, made of blond wood.

"These rooms are pretty nice, aren't they?" Lisa said. "Now, there's a closet you'll share with Bronya—"

"My roommate?" Jill asked.

Lisa nodded. "She should be back from her morning practice any minute, in fact. And here's your bed, your dresser, and a desk. Everything should be empty. The girl who used to be in this room had to go home because of an illness in the family," Lisa continued. "I'll leave you alone to get settled. After your trip you probably want to wash up. The bathroom's down the hall to the left. Remember, if you have any questions, just knock on my door, anytime!"

"Thanks," Jill said. After Lisa left, she sat on her bed and pulled the information packet the Academy had sent her out of her knapsack. The Aspen House, where she was living, was one of two dorms—the other, called the Glacier House, was for boys. There were thirty students at the academy, nineteen girls and eleven boys. And there were ten coaches, each one with a different area of skating expertise. Meals were served in a separate dining hall in the Academy's lodge. Dinner was at six, and her first practice would be the next morning. From Monday through Saturday she would have a two-hour morning practice, then classes with a tutor from nine to one, and then practice again from two to five. Practice with Silver Blades had been demanding, too, but it was nothing like this.

I'm not even going to have time to miss anyone, she thought, standing up to wander around the room.

Whoever her roommate was, she hadn't brought much of her own from home. The walls were practically bare.

Jill couldn't wait for her luggage to arrive. She'd packed a pile of photos of her friends and her family and her favorite skating posters. Once she decorated the room, it would feel more like home. Jill opened the closet and looked at the skating dresses hanging inside. They were plain and tiny—even tinier than Tori's, and Tori was only four foot ten.

"What are you doing?"

Jill whirled around and saw a short girl with light brown hair in a bun standing in the doorway. She laughed nervously. "Hi! You must be my roommate."

The girl gave her a suspicious look. "Are you Jill?" Her accent reminded Jill of Ludmila's.

"Yeah, that's me." Jill smiled. "And you're . . . Bronwyn?"

"Bronya," the girl corrected her. "Bronya Comaneau."

"Bronya. I'm sorry." Jill stepped out of the closet. "I was just looking at all your skating dresses. They're really pretty."

Bronya nodded briefly, acknowledging the compliment.

"So how long have you been here?" asked Jill. "Where are you from?"

"I came three years ago," Bronya said, "from Rumania."

"Wow," Jill said. "That's cool. Rumania is in Eastern Europe, isn't it? So how do you like it here?" She took some things out of her carry-on bag and started putting them on the empty dresser.

"It's okay." Bronya tossed her duffel bag on to the bed, then sat at her desk.

Jill waited for Bronya to say something more, but

Bronya only opened a math textbook and started to read.

She's not very friendly, Jill thought. Maybe she's just shy. I guess I'll have to do the talking. "You must be pretty good if you've been studying with Ludmila for so long," she said. "I can't wait to see you skate. My first practice is scheduled for tomorrow morning. The morning practices are at six, right?"

"Yes, but some people skate at different times," Bronya said, scanning the textbook. "It all depends on your schedule."

Jill nodded. "So . . . what kind of music do you like?" she asked as she unpacked her Walkman. "I'm really into hip-hop. I love to dance."

"I like classical," Bronya said.

"Oh. Well, okay." Jill stacked her cassette tapes on her desktop. She didn't know what to make of her new roommate. Bronya wasn't exactly being rude, but she wasn't being very helpful either. Jill wanted to know all about the school, what to expect, whom to look out for—everything she usually shared with the other skaters at Silver Blades.

She remembered how she had given Nikki advice when Nikki first moved to Seneca Hills and was trying out for the club. She'd tried to encourage Nikki and make her feel at home. That was what Jill needed now. Instead she had Bronya, who was the quietest person Jill had ever met. How was she going to find out anything if Bronya wouldn't talk to her?

Early the next morning Jill took a deep breath and walked out into the arena from the changing room. The rink looked ten times more beautiful than it had in the brochure. The ice looked brand new, as if a Zamboni had just cleaned it, and the lighting was mostly natural—there were skylights in the ceiling to let in the Colorado sunshine. Flags from various countries hung at both ends of the rink, and ,there were indoor trees on both sides too. Jill had never seen a rink that was so gorgeous. Just looking at it made her want to skate her best.

She leaned against the barrier and watched some of the other girls skate. There were eight skaters and three coaches on the ice. Ludmila stood in a corner of the rink, talking to a girl named Meredith, whom Jill had met briefly at dinner the night before. Since Bronya had chosen a table for them in the far corner of the dining room, Jill was only able to meet one or two kids.

Jill saw Bronya at the other end of the rink executing a perfect triple salchow into a double toe loop. "Amazing." She sighed. For such a small girl, Bronya got incredible height on both jumps.

"Don't be too impressed. She's a show-off actually," a boy who had come up beside Jill muttered.

Jill turned to him, surprised. "Who?"

"Bronya," he said. "She seems to think that being European makes her automatically great."

"And who are you?" Jill asked. Bronya wasn't exactly her best friend, but something about this boy's tone made Jill want to defend her.

"Kevin Olsen. You're new here, right? I've never seen you before." He patted her on the shoulder. "Well, don't worry, you'll do fine."

Jill gently removed his hand from her shoulder. "I'm sure I will."

"Well, whatever you do, drink lots of water, or the altitude will really get to you," Kevin advised. "When I first got here, I got these monster headaches. But did Simon accept them as an excuse? No way. 'Kevin, my boy, that's not acceptable.' " He imitated Simon's British accent.

Jill laughed, in spite of the fact that this guy seemed like a jerk. "So when did the headaches go away?"

"When Simon left me alone," Kevin joked. "No, not really. I only had them for the first couple of days— then I got used to the thin air."

"Good," Jill said. "The last thing I need is headaches. I get the feeling things are going to be hard enough without that."

"It's not that bad," Kevin said with a shrug. "I mean, as long as you don't mind being in jail." He smiled, and Jill suddenly noticed that he was very good-looking. He had huge brown eyes and his dark hair was slicked back with gel. Jill guessed he was her

age or a year older. When he smiled, his whole face
lit up.

"I'd better get over there—it's my turn to practice,"
Jill told him.

"Okay—see you later." Kevin threw his jacket over
his shoulder and walked out of the rink.

He's not such a bad guy, Jill thought as she sat
down to lace her skates. At least he talks. And he's
cute.

Her skates laced, Jill stood up and saw Ludmila get
a refill of hot tea from a thermos.

"What are you waiting for?" Ludmila called across
the ice. She waved her arm in a circular motion,
indicating that Jill should come toward her.

Jill took off her skate guards, stepped onto the ice,
and skated over to Ludmila. "Hi," she said. "It's nice
to see you again."

"It's nice to see you too," Ludmila replied. "How
was your trip? Everything all right?"

Jill nodded. "Everything's great, thanks."

"Good. Now, let's begin." Ludmila set her mug of
tea on top of the barrier. "I will not normally be
your coach, Jill, but since you are a new student,
today I will be working with you. Please do some
warm-up work, and then I want to see your spins and
jumps. Afterward I'll have you run through your old
competition program."

Jill nodded. She had stretched out in the changing room before putting on her skates. Now she

started circling the rink, stretching out her legs, taking smooth strokes as she got used to the feel of the ice.

She stopped in front of Ludmila. "What would you like to see first?"

"A back camel spin."

Jill performed several backward crossovers and then transferred her weight to her left foot and swung her right leg around in the air. She leaned forward, carefully keeping her back arched and her chin up, and spun on the ball of her left foot. She made sure she kept her arms straight out on both sides of her. She concentrated on keeping the same pace throughout the spin.

"All right. Let's see your sitspin," Ludmila said next.

Jill went into her sitspin, one of her favorite spins. Building up speed, she lowered her body into a sitting position, held her arms out in front of her, and spun on her left foot, extending her right leg.

"Forward layback," Ludmila said, without commenting on Jill's sitspin. "Use your whole body this time. Make it graceful."

Jill went into a forward layback, but she didn't have enough speed and fell out of the spin too early.

"Terrible!" Ludmila shouted. "You should be well beyond that kind of sloppiness by now."

Jill's face reddened. I can't believe I just did that, she thought, miserable with embarrassment. She glanced at a few of the other girls who had come onto the rink and were also practicing their spins for other coaches. She hoped they hadn't noticed how Ludmila had shouted at her. But everyone was concentrating so intensely on their own spins that no one even looked at her.

At Silver Blades, Jill knew, someone would have given her a sympathetic smile. But there seemed to be no time for that here.

"Come on, Jill—focus!" Ludmila urged.

Jill felt like running from the rink all the way back to Seneca Hills. But instead she took a deep breath and tried the spin again.

6

"**C**hicken or vegetarian stir fry?" the woman behind the buffet counter in the dining hall asked Jill.

Jill stared at the food behind the clear plastic guard. She was so tired, she could barely stay awake. "Chicken, I guess." She took the plate from the top of the buffet. *Not exactly like Mom's home cooking,* she thought, *but it looks okay.* "Thanks." Jill picked up a salad, some bread, a big piece of chocolate cake, and a glass of spring water to drink. Then she looked around the lodge's dining room, hoping to see a familiar face.

She headed over to a table where Bronya sat with a couple of girls she thought she'd seen in her dorm. "Hi," she said, setting down her tray. "What's up?"

"Hello," Bronya said shyly. She turned to the other girls and said, "This is my new roommate, Jill Wong."

"Hi," Jill said. She waited for the other two girls to introduce themselves, but they just nodded and half smiled at her. One of them was very pretty, with long blond hair. The other had wavy black hair that she wore in a short, thick ponytail.

"You two live on my floor, don't you?" Jill asked, hoping this would prompt them into telling her their names.

The blond girl didn't even look at her, but the dark girl said, "Uh-huh. We live next door to you."

Jill looked to Bronya for help, but Bronya was busy eating her stir fry. "Um, I'm sorry, but I don't know your names," Jill said.

The blond girl continued to ignore her. The dark girl said, "Oh. I'm Marie LaFontane. And this is Sarah Miller, my roommate."

"Cool watch," Jill said, pointing to Sarah's plastic watch.

Sarah turned and looked at Jill as if she'd just noticed her presence. Instead of thanking her for the compliment, she brusquely asked, "How old are you?"

Startled, Jill answered, "I'm thirteen. How old are all of you?"

"I'm fourteen," Bronya offered quietly. Jill was surprised. Bronya was tiny and looked about ten.

"Sarah and I are both fifteen," said Marie.

There was another long silence.

Why is everyone around here so hard to talk to? Jill wondered as she spread some butter on a piece of bread. "So what do you like to do—besides skate, I mean?" she asked. She looked at Marie and Sarah and smiled. Sarah kept her eyes on her plate, and Marie glanced at Jill but didn't return the smile.

Bronya gave her a slight smile. Jill was glad that someone appreciated her joke.

"I don't know," Marie said. "At this point I don't think about much else besides my skating. I do plan on making senior Regionals next month."

"Wow," Jill said. "That's pretty impressive."

Marie shrugged. "I guess."

Sarah suddenly turned to Jill again. "How long have *you* been skating?" she asked.

"Since I was eight," Jill said as she began to eat her slice of chocolate cake.

"And she *still* doesn't know how to pick up all those roses from her fans without falling over," Kevin said.

Jill turned around and saw him standing behind her. "Hey, you haven't even seen my curtsies and bows yet," she said with a laugh.

"Call it intuition. So what's the deal?" Kevin pulled out a chair next to Jill and sat down. "I see you're eating. Good, that's good."

Jill gave him a curious look. "What do you mean?"

"Well, things can't be too awful if you're eating," Kevin said.

"You don't know what a big appetite I have," Jill told him.

"You're lucky you're tall, or you could never eat that

much—especially chocolate cake—and stay competitive," Marie said.

Jill looked at her and then at Kevin. He rolled his eyes. "Right. So anyway, how did your practice go?"

This is more like it, Jill thought. Someone who actually *wants* to talk to me. "Not too great. Ludmila doesn't even give you a second to breathe."

"That can be a problem," Kevin said, nodding. " 'But Ludmila,' " he said in a Russian accent, " 'I could not finish my spin because I was out of oxygen!' "

Bronya giggled. Marie and Sarah exchanged glances and stood up.

"Excuse us," said Marie. "We've got to get going."

"But you've hardly eaten anything," said Bronya.

"We're not hungry," said Marie. "See you later, Bronya."

Jill, Kevin, and Bronya watched them go.

"What was that all about?" Jill asked. "Does Marie always do all Sarah's talking for her?"

Bronya shrugged. "They're usually lots of fun," she said.

"Yeah, if you like hanging out with robots," Kevin said dryly. Jill giggled. At least she had *one* person on her side.

Dear Tori, Danielle, and Nikki,
*   I hope you guys don't mind that I'm writing*

you all at the same time, but I'm really exhausted and I want to get this in the mail tomorrow. One letter is better than none, right? I wish I could afford to call you. I can't believe I saw you guys yesterday morning at the airport—it feels like a week ago.

I have to go to bed in a few minutes because my roommate's serious about going to sleep by nine. Can you believe it? Nine? Well, I'm pretty tired anyway, so I guess it's okay.

I had my first practice today, and let's just say that this is going to be a lot harder than I thought. If Kathy is the Sarge, then Ludmila is the General. She didn't like anything I did—she said my spins were sloppy and my jumps looked like a beginner's. It's hard adjusting to a new rink, plus I was nervous. Tomorrow should be better.

I haven't really made any friends yet. It seems like all the girls are either younger or older than me, and a couple of them were really rude to me today. My roommate, Bronya, is shy, make that extremely shy, but I'm working on her. Pretty soon she'll be dancing on the tables in the dining room. I guess I'll get to know other people eventually. I did meet this guy named Kevin Olsen, who's really funny. I think we'll probably hang out a lot together. (He's even cute.)

Write soon and tell me all about what's happening at Silver Blades. Have you picked a theme for the spring show yet? Are you planning the fund-raiser? I wish I could be there to help.

Jill drew a smiling face next to her last comment and signed the letter, "I miss you! Love, Jill." The letter was a lot more optimistic than she felt, but she didn't want anyone to worry about her. Besides, tomorrow *was* going to be better.

As she sealed the envelope, she noticed Bronya was changing into her nightgown. "Time for lights out?" Jill asked.

Bronya nodded.

"I'd better go brush my teeth, then," Jill said. She took her toothbrush, toothpaste, and a towel from her top dresser drawer and started down the hallway to the bathroom.

The bathroom had only two sinks, and both of them were being used—by Sarah and Marie. Sarah looked up when Jill walked in. Then she went back to washing her face.

"Hi," Jill said. She sat on the windowsill to wait her turn. She didn't think it would be long, since Marie was already drying her face with a towel. But then she put the towel down and turned on the water. She splashed her face, then washed her hands. Then she splashed her face again.

Now Sarah began to brush her teeth. Jill watched her brush her top teeth, then her bottom teeth, then her top teeth again, then her bottom teeth again.

Ten minutes passed, and Sarah and Marie were still hogging the sinks.

Jill got up off the windowsill. "Would you mind if I just ducked in here to brush my teeth?" she asked Sarah. "Bronya really wants to go to bed, and I don't want to keep her up."

Sarah acted as if she hadn't heard a word Jill said. She just kept on brushing her teeth.

"Marie?" said Jill. "Can I just wet my toothbrush for a second?"

"Can't you see we're using the bathroom now?" Marie snapped. "You'll just have to wait until we're finished."

Jill stared at them. She could feel her face turning red, and for a second she thought she would start crying. Don't give them the satisfaction, she told herself. Then, without saying a word, she turned and left the bathroom and went back to her room.

Bronya was already in bed with her light out. Jill quickly changed into the big red T-shirt she slept in, got into bed, and turned out her own light.

In the darkness Jill lay perfectly still, but she didn't feel sleepy. It was so quiet in the dorm. She missed her brothers and sisters. She missed her parents. She missed her friends. Everyone here seemed so cold.

Sarah and Marie were clearly being mean to her on purpose. But why? What did they have against her?

Then Bronya said, "Jill? Are you all right?"

"Yeah," Jill said. "I'm okay. But thanks."

"For what?" asked Bronya.

"For asking," said Jill.

She reached under the bed and pulled out Randi's old teddy bear, hugging it closely as she snuggled down under the covers.

"**J**ill, this is your new coach, Holly Abbott," Ludmila said on the ice Tuesday morning. "Holly is our expert at teaching jumps, and I think she can help you with yours."

"Great," Jill said, smiling at Holly. "I can definitely use some help." Jill knew that Holly, who was British, had finished third in the European championships about six years ago. Holly looked nice. She was small, with short blond hair, a pixie nose, and piercing blue eyes. Maybe if she was a little easier on Jill than Ludmila and Kathy had been, it would help Jill finally master her double axel.

Holly led Jill over to the part of the rink that would be theirs for practice.

"So, Jill, how's everything going so far?" Holly asked with a smile.

"Okay, I guess," Jill said. "I'm glad to be here. I've seen tapes of your skating—you're really fantastic."

"Thank you. Now, down to business. All right." Holly looked Jill up and down. "Ludmila tells me you're having trouble landing your double axel."

Holly's intense gaze made Jill feel uncomfortable. "Right," she said, slowly nodding.

"Show me," Holly said. "Stay on this side of the rink. Don't think about anything else, just preparation. Build up speed, and when you are ready, try it."

They sure don't fool around at this place, Jill thought as she skated off to prepare for the jump. It's always, "Nice to meet you. Get to work."

But that's what I came here to do, she reminded herself. She told herself to focus. She was never going to land the jump if she didn't stop thinking about the coaches and what they were thinking about her. She reviewed the jump in her mind, keeping her arms relaxed as she kicked her right leg forward. Then she immediately brought her arms in close to her body as she sprang into the air. She finished the two and a half rotations—but once again she landed on her back inside edge and lost her balance. Jill put her hands on the ice to keep from falling all the way down.

"You barely made two rotations," Holly said. "You need to pull your arms and legs in much tighter. Also don't overrotate your shoulders when you take off."

Jill nodded. She'd heard the same thing before. She

always seemed to swing her arms and shoulders too much on jumps. She prepared for the jump again. The second time she turned only slightly farther before slipping out of the jump—and landing on her rear end.

"Watch your timing," Holly said. "Scoop your arms into your chest at the precise moment you take off and spring." Holly demonstrated the takeoff. "And use your strength, Jill. I know you've done weight training. Don't be afraid."

Jill nodded and tried the double axel again. This time she got enough height to complete the rotations in time, but she landed on her right back inside edge instead of the outside edge as she was supposed to. She lost control of the jump and fell onto the ice.

Landing on my rear end is starting to feel familiar, she thought as she got to her feet again. Usually when she was having trouble with a jump, Kathy would let her try something else after a while and then go back to it. Not Holly. She had Jill try the jump at least twenty more times.

Each time Jill launched into her takeoff. She got plenty of height, but she was so exhausted that she just couldn't make her body turn fast enough. On her last attempt she only finished two rotations before she came back down, her right skate sliding out from underneath her. She fell onto the ice with a loud thud.

When she got up and brushed off her skating skirt, Holly skated over to her. "That's enough for today.

We'll work on something else tomorrow morning. Since I'm going to be your full-time coach, I'll get you a schedule of what times we'll have lessons each day." Then Holly added, "Are you feeling okay? You seem tired."

"I guess I am," Jill said. "I think it's just from getting used to a new place and everything." She didn't want to tell Holly that she was very discouraged.

"I know it's hard," Holly said. "Try to get to sleep early tonight, and I'll see you later. We'll work on spins."

Jill nodded. "Okay. We can work on the jump again tomorrow, right?" She smiled at Holly. As tired and discouraged as she felt, she wasn't about to let anyone think they'd made a mistake in choosing her for the school.

"Right," Holly said. "I like your attitude."

"Okay, everyone—settle down." Ludmila stood at the front of the large meeting room that was on the second floor of the Academy's lodge, right above the dining room. It was Friday night, and Jill couldn't believe she had been at the Academy for four days already. "It's time to start our videotape review."

Ludmila had told Jill about the weekly review. Each member of the Academy was videotaped during practice, and every Friday night they all got together to watch the tapes—and learn from their mistakes.

"Since we have a new member, I want to introduce her to the group," Ludmila said. "This is Jill Wong, from the Silver Blades skating club in Pennsylvania."

Ludmila pointed to Jill, who was sitting at the back of the room, beside Bronya. The rest of the group applauded. Jill saw Kevin smiling at her from across the room.

"We're glad to have you here," Ludmila said.

"Thanks," Jill said. This is more like it, she thought.

"All right—let's get down to business. Roll the tape, please," Ludmila instructed.

The lights dimmed, and a skater appeared on the large television screen. Ludmila took a seat just to the right of the TV, and Simon sat on the left. They started with the boys, and Simon pointed out what each of them was doing right and what each of them had done wrong during that afternoon's practice. Jill fidgeted in her chair, awaiting her turn. Simon made a few funny comments now and then, and the younger girls sitting in front of Jill giggled. One of them reminded her of Randi, with her pigtails and her funny laugh. Jill felt a pang of homesickness and tried by focusing on the screen to push it out of her mind.

When Simon began reviewing Kevin's tape, Jill leaned forward with interest. On the tape Kevin sprang into a triple Lutz and landed it perfectly. He was a very dramatic skater, who'd obviously had a lot of dance and ballet training. He used his arms and his entire body to create a sense of ease in his skating, making the jumps look natural, effortless. He's great, Jill thought.

But Simon was shaking his head. "Kevin, Kevin, Kevin. I've told you a hundred times to pull your arms in tighter on your triple toe loop. You win this week's sloppy award—and last week's, and the week before. . . ."

Several people started laughing, and Jill stared at the tape. Simon was right—at first glance Kevin's jumps looked great, but when she studied each move, she saw that he was slightly imprecise. He was very flashy, but underneath the flash there were errors.

I'm not going to get away with anything here, Jill realized. But she hadn't really expected otherwise.

Simon finished reviewing the male skaters, and Ludmila began discussing the girls. Jill glanced around the room, matching each girl on the tape with the girls in the room. There were girls who looked as if they were about eight years old and girls who looked eighteen. There were nineteen of them in all.

"Tracy, your double flip is coming along nicely," Ludmila said. Tracy, the girl on the tape, was sitting right in front of Jill—and she looked as if she was only nine years old!

I didn't land my double flip until I was twelve, Jill thought. And Nikki and Tori only got theirs consistently this year!

Jill felt a poke in her ribs. "You're next," Bronya whispered.

"Thanks." Jill sat up straighter in her chair and

focused on the screen. She wiped her sweaty palms on her black stretch pants as she watched a girl with long black hair run through a familiar sequence of jumps and spins. She barely recognized herself. It was her first practice session at the Academy.

"Jill!" Ludmila pointed to the screen and hit the slow-motion button. "This is totally incorrect. Your body is all wrong here! Look at that. You're traveling all the way back to Pennsylvania on that combination spin!"

In front of her Jill saw Marie and Sarah whisper to each other, and then they laughed.

Ludmila pointed to Jill's skates. While spinning, a skater wanted to keep her skates in as tight a circle as possible on the ice. Jill had moved several inches to the right. She sank down in her seat, feeling her heart pound with nervousness. They're laughing at *me*! she thought. How humiliating!

"The judges will kill you on that! Your arms—they're not straight enough either," Ludmila went on. "Oh, no. Not like that. Watch your leg—no, no, *no*!"

Sarah and Marie snickered again.

Jill had never heard so much criticism all at once before. Ludmila found fault with nearly everything she did, and she was pointing it out in front of everyone in the whole school. Jill wanted to die.

"So *that* was a lot of fun," Kevin said to Jill after the video session. There were snacks laid out in the dining room downstairs in the lodge—fruit and cookies—and all of the skaters were milling around, talking.

"I'd rather have my teeth pulled without Novocain," Jill told him, taking an oatmeal raisin cookie.

"She did kind of rake you over the coals," Kevin said. He took a sip of hot chocolate. "But she does that to everyone when they first get here. She probably thinks it will motivate you."

"What—humiliate people and they'll improve?" Jill asked.

"Come on, she trashed everyone else too," Kevin said. "You'll get used to it after a while. Did you hear Simon calling me a windup toy stuck at the wrong speed?"

Jill smiled. "That was pretty funny."

"Oh, I get it—it's okay to laugh at *me*," Kevin teased.

"Hi!" a girl with short blond hair said, walking up to Jill. She looked about fourteen. "My name's Bridget. How's it going?"

"Pretty good," Jill said.

"Welcome to the Academy," Bridget said.

"You sound like the stupid brochure," Kevin joked. "Are you going to tell her about the lush grounds next?"

Bridget just looked at him and shook her head. "So what's good to eat? Same cookies and fruit as always?"

"Well, we're giving the hot chocolate a four-point-five," Kevin said. "Lukewarm performance, no style.

The oatmeal cookies get a five-point-one. Technical merit is fine, but no visible nutritional merit."

Jill laughed.

"And you can see how the timing was way off with the picking of these oranges." Kevin made a tsk-tsk noise with his tongue. "You're really going to have to work on that," he scolded the oranges. "You'll never get away with that in a real competition. I mean, dining room."

"Absolutely not," Jill said, giggling. "Back to practice, all of you."

"You guys are weird, you know that?" Bridget laughed and walked over to talk to some of the other boys.

"Too bad we don't get points on weirdness," Kevin said.

"Yeah, you'd get a six," Jill told him. "It could make up for all that sloppy stuff."

"Ha!" Kevin looked mortally offended. "This from the only girl to be called for traveling in a *non*-basketball game!"

Jill laughed again. It felt good to be letting off some steam with Kevin.

Half an hour later Jill walked back to the dorm with Bridget.

"How do you like it here so far?" Bridget asked her.

"It's pretty tough," Jill replied. "But I'm slowly getting the hang of things and getting to know people. Kevin seems like a really nice guy."

When Bridget didn't answer right away, Jill added, "And he's really cute too—don't you think?"

Bridget still said nothing. What is it with these people? Jill thought. Why are they always clamming up on me?

Then Bridget spoke. "Jill," she said, "I wouldn't get too close to Kevin if I were you."

Jill stopped short. "Why not?"

Bridget lowered her voice. "You mean, you really don't know?" she said. "You haven't heard the dirt on Kevin?"

"What dirt on Kevin?" asked Jill.

They were just outside the dorm. Suddenly Lisa, the dorm parent, stepped outside and called, "Girls, let's go! It's almost time for lights out!"

Bridget shrugged. "I'll tell you some other time," she said.

What could it be? Jill wondered as the two girls hurried inside. Kevin had seemed arrogant at first, but actually he was a lot of fun—what could be so bad about him? She hoped she wouldn't have to give up the only friend she'd made since she arrived.

8

Bronya was getting ready for bed when Jill came into the room. Jill closed the door behind her and began to get undressed.

"Bronya," she said, "what do you know about Kevin?"

"Kevin? Well, he's a good skater, but sloppy. . . ."

"That's not what I mean," Jill said. "I was just talking to Bridget, and she told me not to get too close to him, but she didn't tell me why. Do you know why she'd say something like that?"

Bronya nodded. "I think I can guess. It's just that he's been to a lot of skating schools. . . ."

"What's wrong with that?" asked Jill.

"Well"—Bronya seemed uncomfortable—"it's just a lot of gossip, really, but people say he was kicked out of the other schools."

"Kicked out? I wonder why."

"I really don't know," said Bronya. "The way people gossip at this school, it's hard to know what to
believe. And Bridget is one of the worst for spread-
ing rumors. Last year she overheard Simon talking
to Matt, another coach, about how Simon and his
ice-dancing partner were going to Norway on a pro-
fessional skating tour. Except that when Bridget got
through telling everyone, she had the whole Academy
convinced that Simon was running away to Norway
to get married!"

Jill let this sink in. Maybe there wasn't anything
to the rumor of Kevin's being kicked out of schools.
Bridget was probably all wrong about him.

She glanced at her clock. She still had a few minutes before lights out, so she sat at her desk and
picked up the letter she'd gotten that afternoon from
Danielle. It was full of news about her three friends,
as well as about the spring show, and how none of the
members of Silver Blades could agree on a theme for
it.

"Jill, you've got to come up with something,"
Danielle wrote. "There's a big meeting in a couple
of weeks, and we're supposed to have a theme by
then, or else Mr. Weiler says he'll choose one for
us—and we don't want that! Tori, Nikki, and I are
planning to call you two weeks from Saturday; we're
hoping you'll have some ideas. It's the least you can
do since you deserted us. Just kidding! I miss you
and hope you're doing okay. Love, Dani."

Jill picked up a pen and started writing.

＞＿ ＿✍

Dear Dani,

Thanks tons for your letter today. I needed it. Today was both great and terrible at the same time. First the terrible: Tonight I was completely humiliated in front of everyone. We all watched videotapes of each other, and Ludmila made me feel like I had only started skating yesterday. It was totally embarrassing.

Now the good, or maybe I should say the sort-of good. There was a snack break after the video fiasco, and I had a great time with Kevin, who's hysterical (you'd love him) and who made me feel a lot better about being here. Actually I think I may have a crush on him! Can you believe it—me, Jill Wong, interested in a boy! Don't tell anyone else at home yet, okay? I don't know if Kevin likes me back or not. But here's the juicy gossip—he's been kicked out of a lot of skating schools—or at least that's what people say. I wonder why? I hope it isn't true. Kevin is the only fun person I've met in the whole school.

What's happening with the spring show? Why can't you all agree on something? It just has to be springy. What about baseball? You could all sing "Take Me Out to the Ice Rink." No, that's dumb. Maybe something with flowers? I'll work on it. I'll definitely have something by the time you call.

Jill stopped writing and tapped her pen against the desk. She really missed her friends and being part of Silver Blades. With Nikki, Tori, and Danielle, Jill felt as if she was needed, as if she belonged. Here she felt like a stranger.

I'd give anything to be back in Seneca Hills right now, planning the spring show, she thought, instead of working on a new, tough program out here by myself.

She signed the letter and folded it carefully before putting it into the envelope. No one is forcing you to stay in Colorado, Jill, she told herself. You're here because you want to be here—right?

"I see what you're doing," Holly said one afternoon a week later. "When you take off, you're swinging your arm across your body, like this." She demonstrated what Jill was doing wrong. "Watch my arms on takeoff."

Holly showed Jill the correct position of the arms, going from one double axel to the next. Jill watched, awed by how effortless she made the jump look. "Now you try," Holly said.

Jill's first effort wasn't successful—neither was the second. But on her eighth try, just when she was about to give up hope, Jill managed to keep her arms from swinging. She felt herself spring into the air more cleanly and quickly. Before she knew what was happening, she had landed the jump! She was so shocked that she almost fell down anyway.

"All right, then! Good." Holly's face lit up, and she smiled at Jill. "Now I want you to do some mental imaging tonight. Remember how your body felt, how you felt when you made that successful landing. Picture yourself doing that, repeatedly."

"Shouldn't we do some more right now?" asked Jill. She felt like leaping into the air, she was so happy. She felt as if she could do ten consecutive double axels.

"No, I don't think so. You've done enough skating for today, and I want you to leave the ice with a positive feeling. That way you'll come back tomorrow and do the same thing again."

"Okay," Jill said, smiling. "Whatever you think is best."

"I'll go tell Ludmila we made some progress," Holly said. "See you tomorrow, then."

Some progress? Jill couldn't believe it. Only a week after coming to Denver she'd already landed a double axel.

When Jill went into the dressing room, she thought nothing could ruin her good mood—not even Marie and Sarah. The two girls were changing their clothing and barely looked at Jill as she entered. "Hey, guys, what's up?" Jill said cheerfully.

Sarah and Marie just looked at each other.

Jill shrugged and started changing. She wasn't going to let them bother her, not today.

Then Sarah said, "Did you just finish your lesson with Holly?"

Jill nodded. "I'm still in a state of shock. I actually managed to land my double axel today."

"No kidding," Sarah said in a cool voice.

"Yeah," Jill said. "I've been working on it nonstop since I got here."

"How many times did you land it?" Sarah asked.

"Just once," said Jill. "I'm going to work on it again tomorrow."

Marie smirked. "That explains it. It was a fluke."

Jill stared at her. What was that supposed to mean?

"It was no fluke," she told Marie firmly. "Just watch me land it again tomorrow." She grabbed her things and hurried out of the changing room. I'm not about to let those two ice princesses ruin my first good day, she thought, smiling at the term *ice princesses*. Kevin will laugh when I tell him about it, she thought, because that's exactly what Marie and Sarah are: ice princesses.

Time to celebrate! Jill thought as she returned to her room after practice. She was still walking on air after landing her double axel, and she felt like dancing. She picked out her favorite hip-hop tape, popped it into the cassette player, and pressed PLAY. The music poured out, and Jill moved to the beat.

Ten minutes later someone knocked, the door opened, and Lisa came in. "Hi, Jill," she said over the music. "Listen—do you mind turning that off?"

Jill switched the tape player off. Lisa said, "I'm sorry about that, but Sarah wanted me to ask you not to play your music anymore tonight."

Jill was surprised. The music hadn't been that loud. "But it's Saturday night," she said.

"I know," said Lisa. "But Sarah said it was bothering her, and I think we have to respect that. She needs to study."

Jill thought she heard a giggle. She caught a glimpse of Sarah and Marie in the hallway, eavesdropping. Those rats, she thought.

"There must be something fun to do tonight," Jill said to Lisa. "What about a movie? I saw the VCR downstairs. Are we allowed to rent videos?"

"Sure," said Lisa. "That's a great idea. You can ask around at dinner and see if anybody else is interested."

"Great," said Jill. "Thanks, Lisa."

Lisa left, and Jill heard Sarah and Marie giggling again as the door closed behind her.

"So who wants to watch a movie tonight?" Jill asked the girls sitting at her table in the dining room that evening. "Lisa said we could rent a video."

"I don't know," replied Bridget, looking bored. She played with the macaroni and cheese on her plate. "I think I'm going to read."

"How about you, Bronya? Would you like to watch a movie with me?" Jill asked.

Bronya shook her head. "I have to write to my parents. Then I think I'll go to bed early."

Jill wasn't too surprised by that reply at least. Bronya never seemed to want to do anything fun, like watch TV or read magazines. She was completely into her skating, and that was it. No wonder she's so good, Jill thought. That's all she does.

Actually that was all that *anybody* at the Academy seemed to do. They ate, drank, and breathed skating. Don't they ever get sick of it? she wondered.

Jill went over to the juice machine to refill her glass of orange juice. She was startled when she felt someone's hand on her shoulder.

"Hey, what's up?" Jill turned and saw Kevin standing beside her. He held out his glass. "Fill mine up, too, will you?"

Jill raised one eyebrow. "What am I, your waitress?"

Kevin laughed. "Okay, okay, I'll get it myself. So, what are you up to on this thrilling Saturday night?" he asked, rolling his eyes. "Can you stand the excitement around this place?"

Jill smiled faintly. "Actually I was just trying to get someone to rent a movie with me, and they acted like

I wanted them to jump off a cliff. I guess it would be *too* exciting to do something besides think about skating."

"Are you serious? No one wanted to watch a movie?" he asked.

Jill nodded.

"Who needs them anyway?" said Kevin. "I'll watch a movie with you. What kind of movies do you like?"

"I'll watch anything you want," Jill said. "Except skating, that is. Lisa said she'd drive us to the mall to pick something out."

"Excellent," said Kevin. "Then we can come back and watch the movie at your dorm—just the two of us."

"That was seriously bad," Kevin said, pressing the rewind button on the dorm's VCR. "I mean, how could they come up with such a dorky idea?"

Jill laughed. "They should put it in the Comedy section instead of Horror." She watched Kevin put the tape back in the box.

When she'd arrived at the Academy, she never thought she'd be spending all her free time with a boy. But here she was with Kevin—and she was having a lot of fun. She still hadn't had a chance to find out more about "the dirt" on him—whatever it was, it couldn't be that bad, could it? He was such a great guy.

"Now what?" Kevin tossed the video box onto the couch, next to Jill. "What time is it?"

Jill glanced at her watch. "It's only nine. What else is there to do around here?"

Kevin looked at her and raised one eyebrow. "Are you serious?"

"There must be something we could do," Jill said.

"Well—there is something," Kevin said with a mischievous grin. "We could go sledding."

"Sledding—now?"

"Come on, it'll be fun. There's fresh snow on the hill behind the dorm," Kevin coaxed. "And there are sleds and stuff in that closet." Kevin got to his feet and opened the closet door. "See?" He pulled out some red plastic saucers and his coat. "It will be a blast."

"Aren't we supposed to let someone know where we're going first?" Jill asked.

Kevin shrugged. "Come on. Who'll notice?"

"Okay," Jill agreed. After all, Kevin had been here longer than she had and probably knew the ropes. "It's better than sitting in my room with the lights out," she said. "Bronya's probably already asleep by now."

"That's what I like to hear." Kevin held her coat out to her and draped her red scarf around her neck.

Jill giggled as she slipped into her coat. Kevin handed her a saucer, and they went out the front door.

Outside, the air was cold and fresh. Jill looked up at the sky. She'd never seen so many stars.

She started around the dorm toward the back. Suddenly a snowball came whizzing past her ear, just missing her.

"Hey!" she cried. She turned around to see Kevin brushing snow from his hands, trying to look innocent.

"You don't know who you're dealing with, Kevin," she joked. "I'm the snowball champ of Seneca Hills!" She dropped her sled and ran around the side of the dorm. Crouching low to the ground, she quickly packed a snowball together and peeked around the corner at Kevin. She flung the snowball at him. It hit him—*smack!*—right in the chest.

"Bull's-eye!" she cried.

"This means war!" he yelled, scrambling to hide behind a bush. A snowball zinged through the air and hit the side of the dorm, just missing Jill.

"All right, Olsen, you're in big trouble now!" Jill screamed. She hurled a snowball as hard as she could in his direction.

Then there was the sound of smashing glass.

"Oops," Kevin murmured.

"Hey! Who did that?" someone yelled. Jill looked up and saw Sarah's blond head framed by a broken second-floor window.

"Sorry!" Jill called up to her. "I'm really sorry, I didn't mean to hit your window!"

"It was you!" Sarah shouted angrily. "I should have known."

Marie's face appeared beside Sarah's. "It's freezing in here!" she said. "Look at the hole you made!"

"Hey, it was an accident!" said Kevin.

"Right," said Sarah. "As if I should listen to a troublemaker like *you*, Kevin."

"I didn't mean to do it!" Jill called up to them. "I'll come inside and help you clean up."

"Don't you dare!" said Sarah. "You're not setting foot in my room."

"I'm going to get Lisa," said Marie.

"You're going to be in big trouble, Jill," said Sarah. "I hope they kick you out of here." She and Marie moved away from the window.

"I can't believe this," Jill said. She was shaking. "Do you think I'll really get in trouble?"

"What are they going to do—kick you out for breaking one lousy window?" Kevin said. "I don't think so."

"Well, I guess I'd better go in," Jill said. "Thanks for watching the movie with me."

"No problem," said Kevin. "And Jill—don't worry so much. It'll be okay."

"Thanks," said Jill. "See you later." Kevin turned and jogged toward the boys' dorm.

Jill went inside. The door to Lisa's apartment was open, and Jill saw Sarah and Marie sitting on Lisa's couch. Lisa stood in the doorway waiting for her.

"I'm really sorry about the window," Jill began.

"Lisa, it was an accident, it really was. Kevin and I were just fooling around, throwing snowballs."

"You should be more careful," Lisa said. "Someone could have been hurt."

Jill looked at Marie and Sarah, who were both glaring at her.

"It was no accident," Sarah said. "She aimed for our window."

"What?" Jill couldn't believe her ears. "Why would I do something like that? I don't want to hurt either one of you."

"Sarah, did you actually *see* Jill aim for your window?" Lisa asked.

"I didn't have to," said Sarah. "I know she did."

"I'd never do anything like that," Jill insisted. "Why won't you believe me?"

"I'm sure it wasn't intentional," Lisa told them. "These things happen. But I'm afraid Maintenance won't be able to replace the glass until tomorrow"— she turned to Marie and Sarah—"so tonight you'll have to sleep in my apartment."

"Great," Marie said sarcastically.

"Go upstairs and get whatever you need," Lisa said.

"I'm really sorry," Jill said as she followed Marie and Sarah to the second floor.

"You can stop pretending," Sarah said. "We know you did it on purpose."

"You were getting back at us for what we said at the rink today, weren't you?" said Marie. She stopped outside the door to their room.

"Or was it for telling Lisa to get you to stop blasting that horrible music of yours?" said Sarah.

Jill was so amazed, she couldn't reply. What was with these girls? Why did they hate her so much?

"Well, don't worry, Jill," Sarah said. "Maybe Lisa will let you get away with this—but we won't. Somehow, some way, we'll get you back."

9

Dear Mom,

It's late Sunday morning, and I'm sitting in the dining room here in the lodge eating brunch by myself. We don't have practice on Sunday, so it's a good time to catch up on my letter writing. I wish I could go outside and do something, either go skiing or go into Denver and walk around, but I can't exactly get anywhere on my two little feet, so I guess I'm stuck here.

It's been a pretty uneventful week, thank goodness. I'm definitely getting my double axel down— I can land it at least half the time now. Otherwise, things are pretty calm. Since I broke that window last weekend, I've been extra careful. I don't want to do anything else to upset those two girls who live next door to me. They seem to be just waiting for me to do something wrong. I don't understand it.

How's everyone? Tell them I miss them, and tell Randi I sleep with her teddy bear every night.

Have you seen Tori, Nikki, or Danielle lately? They were supposed to call me yesterday, but they didn't. They asked me to help them come up with a theme for the spring show, and I stayed up really late Friday night trying to come up with something. But then they didn't call. It's not like them.

"Jill, there you are!" Kevin exclaimed, walking into the dining room.

Jill glanced at her watch. "You just made it," she said. "They're about to stop serving brunch."

"I never worry about being late for meals," Kevin said. "They won't let me starve." He sat down beside Jill. She covered her letter with her arm so Kevin couldn't read it.

"Listen," Kevin went on, "I have a plan. In fact it's the best plan I've had in weeks. Want to hear it?"

"Definitely," Jill said. "What's up?"

"Well, the only thing going on today is that meeting at five, right?" Jill nodded. "So how'd you like to go into Denver and wander around—check out some CD stores, buy some stuff, whatever?"

Jill smiled. "That sounds great." She had been wanting to go into the city ever since she got to Colorado. "There's only one problem—how can we go?"

"What do you mean?" asked Kevin.

"Number one, how do we get permission?" Jill couldn't imagine Ludmila letting her and Kevin wander around by themselves in the middle of Denver. "And number two, it's about a half hour's drive from here, isn't it?" Jill asked.

"There's a bus we can take," Kevin said. "One of those commuter deals that runs on the weekends too. We can walk to the bus stop from here."

"Okay, but you didn't answer my first question."

"Look, it's called free hours, isn't it?" asked Kevin. "Doesn't that mean we can do whatever we want?"

"I guess so," said Jill. "But I think we should tell someone where we're going."

"I already did," Kevin said. "I stopped by your dorm and told Lisa, and then I talked to Scott." Scott was the boys' dorm parent. "They both said it was fine."

"But I thought we weren't supposed to take off on our own," Jill said. "Isn't someone supposed to come with us?"

"But we won't be on our own—we'll be there together," Kevin said. "That's all they mean by that. The old buddy system."

"Are you sure?" Jill asked.

"Positive. Listen, the next bus leaves at eleven-thirty," Kevin said. "If we hurry, we can make it."

Jill stuffed her pen and the unfinished letter into her knapsack and quickly checked to make sure she had her wallet. "Then let's go!"

"It feels so good to get away from the dorm," Jill said. She and Kevin were sitting at an outdoor coffee shop in downtown Denver. "Everybody is so tense there. Marie and Sarah won't let me forget about that stupid broken window. They go out of their way to be mean to me."

"They're out of control," Kevin said, drinking his soda. "I mean, what did you ever do to them?"

Jill shrugged and added some sugar to her iced tea. "Just showed up, I guess. They haven't liked me since the moment I got here."

"Exactly," Kevin said. "It has nothing to do with your personality, believe me. They're probably just jealous because you're better than they are."

"Do you really think I'm better?" Jill had been so busy skating herself, she'd barely had time to notice what everyone else was—or wasn't—doing.

"Yeah, definitely," Kevin said. "You're more graceful. I think if you stick around, you'll end up making it all the way to the Nationals."

"If I stick around? What do you mean?" Jill asked.

"Just that I can see why you might want to leave," Kevin said. "I mean, school's no picnic, and with Ludmila trashing you all the time—"

"It's not that," Jill said. "I can handle that." She sipped her iced tea.

"Yeah, sometimes," Kevin said. "But not when it's

all the time. The coaches are so picky. Simon and Ludmila told me before I came to the Academy that I had all this potential. But now all Simon does is get on my case about every little thing I do wrong on the ice."

Jill thought about it. Ludmila and Holly didn't criticize her *all* the time. It was just that when they did, it really hurt. She wanted so badly to do well.

"And then you've got all the prima-donna ice princesses walking around with their noses in the air," Kevin said. "I've been watching them for the three months that I've been at the Academy. Give me a break! Are we supposed to take these people seriously?"

"I don't know." Jill smiled weakly. "I guess it's all just part of being a skater."

"Well, not all the skating schools are like this, believe me," Kevin said. "I should know."

Jill cleared her throat. This was her chance to find out what was really behind the gossip about Kevin. But she wanted to be tactful about it. "Exactly how many skating schools have you been to?" she asked.

The question didn't seem to bother Kevin at all. "Nine. My dad's been shipping me around for the last five years. The longest I ever lasted at one school was . . . four months, I think."

"Four months? Wow. What made you leave all those places?" asked Jill.

"Sometimes they asked me to," Kevin said. "They said I wasn't putting in the effort. But I can't stick to all those rules—it drives me crazy. And sometimes I just left because I got fed up or didn't like my coach or whatever."

Only four months, Jill thought. That wasn't really long enough to give something a chance. Back at Seneca Hills she and Kathy Bart hadn't even begun to work well together until six months after they started. "Well, I'm not going to leave," she told Kevin. "Although I have been wondering when I'm going to start liking it more and have some fun."

"Aren't you having fun now?" Kevin asked, grinning at her.

"Sure—but we're not *there* now," Jill said.

"Exactly. I told you it was a good plan. Hey, you want to split a piece of cheesecake?"

Jill smiled. "Chocolate chip or cherry?"

"Where *is* he?" Jill grumbled at three forty-five that afternoon. Kevin had taken off on his own when Jill went to try on some clothes in a women's clothing store. He'd promised to meet her in front of a restaurant on Sixteenth Street at three-thirty. They'd planned to catch the three-fifty bus and be back at school by four-thirty, in plenty of time for the meeting at five. But if Kevin didn't show up soon, they were going to miss the bus and be late—very late.

Why did I let Kevin talk me into this? Jill wondered. But it hadn't been hard—she'd wanted to get away from the Academy so badly. Now, though, all she wanted was to get back on time. She didn't want to know what Ludmila was like when she got angry. She had a feeling it wouldn't be a pretty sight.

Jill spotted a telephone on the other side of the street and decided to call Lisa, to tell her they'd be late getting back. She dialed the number and waited for Lisa to pick up, but there was no answer.

Jill started walking down the mall, thinking perhaps she and Kevin had crossed signals somehow. Suddenly she spotted Kevin lingering outside a CD store, staring in the window.

"Kevin! Come on, we have to go!" she called to him.

He casually sauntered over to her. "Hey, what time is it?"

Jill stared at him, then grabbed the sleeve of his jacket and started pulling him toward the bus stop. She turned—and saw the bus, just pulling up to their stop!

"Come on!" she shouted. "There's the bus!"

She and Kevin ran as fast as they could, shouting for the driver to stop. But the bus pulled away from the curb and drove down the street and out of sight.

"Kevin, how could you!" Jill shouted. "We missed our bus, and it's all your fault!"

The expression on Ludmila's face when Jill showed up at the lodge at five-thirty told her everything she needed to know. She was in big trouble. Ludmila didn't say anything when she and Kevin walked in and sat down, but she gave them a look that showed she was clearly angry.

Ludmila was in the middle of describing preparations for an upcoming skating demonstration at the Academy. Jill tried to pay attention, but all she could think about was what Ludmila was going to say to her as soon as the meeting was over.

When Ludmila finished talking, Jill went straight up to the front of the room. She wanted to make the first move. "I'm very sorry I was late," she said. "It was Kevin's fault. He—"

Lisa rushed over to them. "Jill, I was worried about you. What happened? Where were you?"

"Well, Kevin was supposed to meet me to take the bus back at three-fifty, but—"

"The bus? Bus back from where?" Ludmila asked.

"Denver," Jill said.

"Denver?" Lisa said. "You went into Denver by yourselves?"

Jill looked at Lisa. "Didn't Kevin tell you?"

Lisa shook her head. "No. If he had, I would have told him that you're not allowed to go off campus by yourselves. Kevin knows the rules—he just thinks they don't apply to him. He's been trouble from the moment he enrolled in the Academy. But, Jill, you should have at least checked with me."

Jill ran a hand through her hair. "You're right, but Kevin told me he'd okayed it with you. I'm sorry."

"Jill, this is very serious. For one thing it's not safe. If anything happened to you—well, how do you think your parents would feel, if I didn't know where you were?" Ludmila asked Jill.

Jill looked down at the floor. "Pretty terrible."

"So you understand why we have these rules," Ludmila said.

Jill nodded. "Yes, I do."

"You need to know all the rules—don't rely on anyone else to tell you what they are," Lisa said.

"Lisa tells me you had a problem last week, too, breaking a window in your dorm," Ludmila went on.

"I'm sorry for everything," Jill said. "Really, I won't make any more mistakes."

"I hope not. But I'm afraid I can't just let this go. I'm glad you're all right, but things could have turned out very badly," Ludmila said.

Jill stared at her, feeling panicky.

"So I am taking away your privileges. You will not be allowed off the Academy grounds—even with a chaperone—for the next month," Ludmila said. "We'll call it a temporary probation."

Jill heaved a sigh of relief. She hadn't planned on going anywhere anyway. She was glad Ludmila hadn't made her stay away from the rink for a day or something like that. She'd never forgive herself if she'd jeopardized her skating career over something so stupid. "Okay. Thank you," she said softly.

She saw Kevin across the room. Simon and Scott were talking to him in hushed but angry tones. She couldn't believe she had listened to Kevin and that he had lied to her like that. Maybe *he* wanted to get kicked out of school, but she didn't!

"I don't think Kevin really wants to be here," Bronya said as she and Jill sat in their room after dinner that evening. "Maybe you should stay away from him."

"Too late now! I'm already in hot water with Ludmila—and everyone else around here," Jill complained. "I can't believe Kevin—he even had the nerve to tell me he didn't mean for us to get into trouble."

"Maybe he didn't," Bronya said. "Maybe he thought you'd get back in time, before anyone noticed."

"Still . . ." Jill quickly brushed her hair.

There was a knock on the door, and Jill opened it. "Telephone call," Amanda, a younger girl who lived at the other end of the hall, said.

Jill went out into the hall and picked up the phone from the wall. "Hello?"

"Thanks for calling us back!" Tori said sarcastically.

"Yeah!" said Danielle. "We waited all night!"

"And all day today," said Nikki.

"Hi, you guys!" Jill said. She was so glad to hear her friends' voices. "What is this—a conference call? Where are you?"

"We're all on extensions at Tori's house," said Danielle. "What happened yesterday?"

Jill was confused. "What are you talking about? I was waiting for *you* to call *me*."

"We did call you—didn't anyone tell you?" Nikki said.

"We left a message saying you should call us collect whenever you got in. We had a sleepover here and we were waiting up late for you to call."

"I didn't get a message that anyone called," Jill said. "Who did you talk to?"

"I don't know," Tori said. "I didn't ask her name."

"I have a feeling I know who it was," Jill whispered. "There are these two girls on my hall who hate me."

"What do you mean? What happened?" Danielle asked.

"It's kind of a long story. . . ." Jill began. She quickly described everything that had happened with Marie and Sarah and how she'd gotten in trouble with Kevin that day.

"What a creep!" Tori said. "I thought you said Kevin was cool."

"That's what I thought," Jill said with a sigh. "So now I'm on probation. Oh, I wish you guys were here! Nobody here understands me the way you do. I can't seem to do anything right!"

"Well, if it makes you feel any better, we miss you like crazy here," said Danielle.

"So have you come up with a theme for the spring show yet?" Tori asked. "The meeting's tomorrow, you know."

"So far our best idea is 'Spring Break,' " said Nikki. "But Silver Blades used that theme three years ago."

"Actually I did have an idea," Jill said. Just talking to her friends made her feel a little better. "How about 'Spring Romance'? What do you think?"

"I love it!" said Tori.

"It's great," said Danielle. "We'll propose it at the meeting tomorrow. I bet everybody will love it."

"Don't forget to give me credit," Jill joked.

"We won't," said Nikki.

"Listen, don't let those two ice princesses get you down," Tori said.

"Or Kevin either," said Danielle. "I know you'll have lots of real friends soon."

"Thanks, you guys," said Jill. "You're the greatest."
Jill hung up the phone, feeling better. But as she passed Marie and Sarah's room on her way down the hall, she began to feel angry. How could they deliberately not tell her about a phone message? She'd had just about enough from them. She wasn't going to take it anymore.

Jill knocked on their door. Sarah opened it.

"Did you take a phone message from some friends of mine yesterday?" Jill demanded.

Sarah looked back at Marie, who was sitting on her bed. Marie smirked. "Oops. I'm so sorry," she said. "I guess I forgot to tell you."

Jill crossed her arms. "Look—why don't you two just come out and say it—what did I ever do to you? Why don't you like me?"

Sarah and Marie exchanged glances. "We have our reasons," Sarah said.

"Well, I wish you'd tell me what they are," said Jill. "Because all *I've* wanted since I got here was to be friends with everybody—even you. And you've done nothing but smirk and laugh at me and try to get me in trouble. Well, I give up. I'm not going to try to be friends with you anymore. From now on, we're enemies!"

She ran into her room and slammed the door.

"That's it for this week," Ludmila said when she turned off the video player on Friday night.

Jill stood up and stretched her legs. She was glad the evening was almost over. She just wanted to get out of there before Kevin tried talking to her again.

"Jill, could you stay for a minute?" Ludmila asked as Jill passed her on her way out the door. "I need to talk to you."

Great, Jill thought. Don't tell me I'm in trouble again. She slumped down in a chair and waited for everyone to leave the room.

"I know you've been having some problems lately, but this is not about that. I want to know if you noticed anything different about your skating when you watched today's tape," Ludmila said, sitting in a chair opposite her. Holly had also remained in the room.

Jill shrugged. "Just that my jump combinations look a lot better. And I'm still not finishing right on the double axel."

Ludmila brushed at a piece of lint on the sleeve of her black sweater. "This is sometimes very difficult to talk about," she said. "I don't want you to get upset. But what I'm seeing is that—you have no emotion."

Jill sat up straighter in her chair. "What do you mean?" All I have is emotion! I'm homesick, I'm upset . . . she thought.

"I think what Ludmila is talking about is that you don't seem to like skating very much," Holly added. "You've improved quite a bit technically, but—well, when you're skating, you seem kind of lifeless."

"Lifeless?" Jill couldn't believe it. She'd been pouring every ounce of energy she had into her skating. And she'd never been criticized for her lack of emotion before.

"One thing we liked when we saw you in Lake Placid was that you obviously loved performing in front of a crowd," Ludmila continued. "You were a very expressive skater. But now you seem only to be going through the motions."

"And when a skater is not enjoying herself on the ice, it shows," Holly said, looking truly concerned.

"What can I do?" Jill asked. "Smile at the crowd some more?"

"It's not that exactly," Holly said patiently.

"You don't seem very excited about the dramatic progress you've been making," Ludmila said. "You seem—well, unhappy."

All at once Jill felt as if she would burst. All anyone ever did at this school was criticize her!

"I'm *not* happy," she cried. "I hate it here!" She jumped out of her chair and ran out of the room.

Jill tore out of the front door of the main building, past the others who were gathered in the dining hall for the traditional postmeeting fruit and cookies. She ran down the hill toward Aspen House and up the stairs. She didn't stop running until she reached her door. Then she opened it, threw herself on her bed, and burst into tears.

Jill didn't hear anyone come in, but when she looked up from her pillow, there stood Bronya, looking concerned.

"Jill, what's wrong?" Bronya asked, touching Jill's arm gently. "What happened?"

Jill wiped her face on the pillowcase and sat up, trying to catch her breath. She'd been crying so hard, she wasn't even sure if she could talk. "I . . ." She sniffled. "I . . ."

"Was it something Ludmila said to you?" Bronya asked.

Jill nodded, and more tears slid down her face.

"Oh, no. Don't let her upset you so much." Bronya took a tissue from the box on her dresser and handed it to Jill.

Jill blew her nose. "That's easy for you to say. You've been training with her for years. She *likes* you."

"She likes you too," Bronya said. "She just doesn't show it in the usual way. You'll get used to her after a while."

"Bronya, no offense, but you're always saying that," Jill said. "You keep saying I'll get used to it here. But it's been almost a month and I'm *not* getting used to it." She wiped a fresh tear from her eye. "Everything's been going wrong. Marie and Sarah can't stand me; Kevin got me into trouble; now Ludmila and Holly say that my skating stinks. I'm trying my hardest to skate well, but I *can't*. Not with everyone making it so hard for me."

"This school isn't easy. I know that. But you're just having a bad week," Bronya said.

Jill shook her head. "It's not going to change! At home I'm used to having friends and my family around—people who really care about me. Out here everyone's out for themselves."

"Not everyone, just some people," Bronya told her. "Anyway maybe this will cheer you up. Didn't you see this downstairs?" Bronya handed her a big blue envelope.

Jill was amazed that the post office had been able to deliver the letter—the writing on it was so scrawled that she could barely make out her name, never mind her address. She ripped open the envelope and pulled out a piece of construction paper. On it her twin brothers, Michael and Mark, had drawn a picture of Jill in a skating outfit.

"I did the skates," Henry had written at the bottom. In the picture Jill's hair was flying out on all sides, and her legs were as long as tree trunks. "We miss you!" Henry wrote. "Come back."

"It's from my little brothers." Jill held it out and showed Bronya.

"It's very cute," Bronya said, smiling. "I can see why you miss them so much."

Jill felt tears filling her eyes again. She brushed them away and pulled the scrapbook Danielle, Tori, and Nikki had given her off of her desk and stuck the drawing into it.

Jill flipped through the photo album, toying with the silver skate charm necklace she was wearing. Her three friends from home each wore the same necklace. "See this, Bronya? In almost every picture I'm with my friends or my family—and I'm *smiling*. How many times have you seen me smile lately?"

"Well . . . not too many, I have to admit," Bronya said. "But you'll be smiling again soon, I know it. It's just that you're overwhelmed right now. It's hard to leave home and come to a new place. I know. Skating requires a lot of concentration. And it's hard to skate well when you're thinking about something else."

Jill nodded. "I can't stop wishing I were back in Seneca Hills. And I don't know if this feeling is ever going to go away."

"Give it time," said Bronya. "Why don't you just forget today and start over tomorrow."

Jill looked at the letter from her brothers again. Maybe she would start over tomorrow, but it might not be in the way Bronya expected.

Jill double-checked her map in the small pool of light cast by her bedside lamp. As far as she could tell, all she had to do was take the same bus she had taken with Kevin into Denver. From there she could catch a bus to Chicago and then Philadelphia. The bus to Denver left in fifteen minutes.

She glanced across the room where Bronya lay sleeping. Then she closed her small suitcase as quietly as she could. She'd just have to ask Lisa to send the rest of her things when she got home.

She picked up the suitcase and tiptoed to the door. It squeaked a little when she pulled it open.

"Jill? What are you doing?" Bronya asked in a sleepy voice.

Jill looked back and saw Bronya sitting up in bed.

"Where are you going? It's three in the morning! Something bad hasn't happened in your family, has it?" Bronya asked.

Jill shook her head. "No. It's just . . ." She quickly closed the door so that no one would hear them talking and leaned against it. "I decided that I'm going to leave the school."

"What? Leave the school?" Bronya looked shocked. "You can't do that."

"Yes, I can," Jill said. She'd been awake all night planning how she would leave. She didn't want to tell anyone, least of all her parents, who would probably make her stay. She was just going to call them when she got to Chicago and tell them she was on her way. She'd planned to sneak out of the dorm before everyone else was awake.

"You can't do that," Bronya repeated.

Jill had never heard her shy roommate sound so forceful. "Give me one reason why I shouldn't. I don't belong here, and you know it."

"Yes, you do, Jill," Bronya said quietly. "Do you always run away when there are challenges?"

Jill looked at her and shook her head.

"What did you do when you had problems at home?" Bronya asked.

"I worked them out," Jill said. "But there were always people to help me—not like here. Here I feel like everyone's against me, everyone's always trying to get me in trouble."

"Not everyone. People here will help you too," Bronya insisted. "You just have to give them a chance."

Jill sighed. "I don't know, Bronya. I just don't know how to make things better here. It doesn't seem like they're going to change."

"You can start again," Bronya went on. "Part of the problem is you just met the wrong people first. Kevin's nice and fun, but he's not very serious about skating."

Jill nodded. "I know that now," she said. "Hanging out with Kevin gave people the wrong impression of me. I like him a lot, but I guess spending too much time with him isn't a great idea right now."

"Jill, even though I'm always saying that I'm used to the Academy, it's not always easy for me to be here. I'm so far away from my parents. I miss them. And I've given up all my old friends. You get letters almost every day," Bronya said. "But I've been here so long that I'm not friends with anyone back home anymore. You have gotten more letters in three weeks than I have in a year!" She laughed. "Maybe not that bad, but still."

"But on the other hand you have a totally amazing double axel," Jill told her, smiling. "While mine is nonexistent."

"But you just got here," Bronya said. "If you stay, you'll land a double axel, too, eventually. That's why you decided to come to the Academy—to become a championship skater. And that takes time, just like getting used to life at the Academy does. But I don't want you to be miserable. If you still think you should go, I won't try to stop you."

Jill sat on her bed and toyed with the nametag on her suitcase. She remembered her father tying it onto the bag and Randi trying to help him. "I bet this suitcase is going to go to a lot of competitions," he had said. "Even across the Atlantic someday." He had hugged Jill and told her how proud she made him.

Jill didn't know what to do. She had already missed

the bus to Denver. She sighed as she took off her sweater and jeans and put her nightshirt back on and slipped under her covers. She knew Bronya was watching her, waiting for Jill to say something.

"I guess I'll wait until later to decide what to do," she told Bronya quietly. "Maybe things will make more sense then."

Before she turned out the light, Jill took one last look at her packed suitcase. There would be another bus to Denver in the morning.

Jill was relieved when she heard Bronya's alarm clock buzz a couple of hours later at five-thirty. Since she'd climbed back into bed, she'd been tossing and turning, unable to sleep.

But she had made a decision.

She had thought about what Bronya had said. And she'd remembered back to when Kevin had told her that he hadn't stayed in any skating school for more than four months. No wonder his skating hasn't improved, Jill had thought again. He never stays anywhere long enough to make progress. I don't want my skating career to be like that.

Bronya was right, Jill decided. Jill could either stay here and try to become a better skater, or she could go back home to her friends and family, where she knew what to expect, and where everyone was behind her, no matter what.

Jill had always wanted to become a world-class skater, ever since she'd started skating. This is my big chance, and I'm running away just because it's harder than I thought, Jill scolded herself. I've never run away from problems before. Why should I start now?

Bronya got out of bed, stretched, and glanced over at Jill. "So is this good-bye?" she asked.

Jill shook her head. "I've changed my mind."

Bronya's face lit up. "I'm so glad. What made you change your mind?"

"You did," said Jill. "You know what, Bronya? I was wrong. Not only about wanting to leave. About everyone here being against me. You're not. You're a real friend. Thanks."

"It's nothing," Bronya said. "Roommates have to stick together. I learned that from watching Sarah and Marie."

Jill rolled her eyes. "They definitely stick together. I don't think I've ever seen them apart, except during practice."

"It's even worse now that Sarah switched coaches," agreed Bronya. "Now that both she and Marie are working with Matt, sometimes they even practice together."

Jill got out of bed, opened her suitcase, and started unpacking. "I didn't know Sarah had switched coaches. Why did she do that?"

"Ludmila made her switch, about a month ago," said Bronya. "I don't know why. Sarah was really upset."

"Who was Sarah's old coach?" Jill asked.

"Holly," Bronya answered. "A lot of people think Holly is the best coach."

Jill put down the dress she'd been unfolding.

Is that why Sarah hates me? she wondered. Just because of Holly? Sarah can't stay angry about that for *too* long, Jill reasoned. Or could she?

"Jill, I'm glad you're here," Ludmila said when Jill knocked on her office door in the lodge that afternoon before lunch. "I wanted to have a talk with you."

"Me too," said Jill. "Can I come in?"

"Please, sit down." Ludmila gestured toward an empty chair.

"First of all, I'm really sorry I blew up yesterday," Jill said. "I know that you and Holly were only trying to help me."

"That's all right," Ludmila said. "Actually Holly and I wanted to talk with you to see if there was anything we could do to make you feel more at home here. You seem very homesick, and I'm sure that is what's affecting your skating."

"I do miss my family and friends at home a lot. In fact I was ready to leave the Academy for good last night," Jill admitted. Ludmila raised her eyebrows in surprise but remained silent.

"But I changed my mind. I'm going to stay here and really work on my skating," Jill went on. "I realized that I wasn't giving the school much of a chance. I wanted everything to happen fast. All I could think about was how much better things were at home. I wasn't making a real effort to make this my new home."

"That's understandable, especially if you haven't been away from home before." Ludmila cleared her throat. "Jill, there's something else I wanted to talk to you about—a personal matter. I hope you don't mind."

"No," said Jill. "I don't mind."

"Good. Lisa tells me that you haven't been getting along well with Marie LaFontane and Sarah Miller. Quite frankly this surprises me. You seem to be a very friendly girl, and Marie and Sarah have never had problems getting along with the other girls before. Do you know of any reason why you shouldn't get along with them?"

Jill shifted nervously in her seat. "I don't know anything for sure," she said. "But I do have a hunch."

Ludmila nodded.

"Well, Bronya told me that you switched Sarah's coach right before I got here."

"That's right," said Ludmila. "Sarah had been working with Holly for a very long time. I thought it might help her to try working with Matt for a change."

"But I think Sarah thinks you switched her so that *I* could work with Holly instead," said Jill. "It's just a guess, but she's been mean to me ever since I got here."

"That's ridiculous," said Ludmila. "I told Sarah why I was switching her to Matt. We don't have time for that kind of petty nonsense here. Sarah will get over this in time," Ludmila went on. "And now—you are ready to start again?"

"Yes," Jill said, breathing a sigh of relief.

"Good," Ludmila said. "I know there are things about the school that take getting used to—such as the video critiques. I have to admit there are days when I would hate to see *myself* on video!" She laughed. "But I think you'll do fine. Well, I must do some paperwork before lunch. Thank you for coming to see me, Jill." Ludmila looked up and smiled.

"Thanks," said Jill. She left Ludmila's office and headed for the dining room. Now she knew she was right about Sarah—and, much as she dreaded it, she knew what she had to do.

Jill walked into the dining area and scanned the room. Most of the skaters had classes at that hour, so there were only a few people scattered around the tables. Jill spotted Sarah sitting alone at a side table, just as she had hoped. Jill took her tray over and sat down across from Sarah.

"Hi, Sarah," she said. "Mind if I sit here?"

Sarah looked up at her, then quickly back at the book she was reading. "It's a free country," she said.

Jill poked her straw into her milk carton and took a sip. This was going to be hard, she knew. And maybe it wouldn't work. But she had to try. She couldn't stand living next door to someone who hated her.

"Listen, Sarah," she began. "I just wanted you to know that—well, I'd be upset too."

"What are you talking about?" Sarah asked without looking up.

"I'm talking about Holly," Jill said. "I know that she used to be your coach. . . ."

Sarah looked up now, her face angry. "You have some nerve, you know that?" she said in a low voice. "Do you think you're so great, Ludmila would switch coaches around just for you? I *asked* to work with Matt, if you want to know the truth."

Jill blanched. "I'm sorry," she said. "From what Bronya told me, I just assumed. . . . Well, I kind of thought the two of us were going through the same thing."

"You and I have nothing in common," said Sarah.

"Maybe we do," said Jill. "Back in Pennsylvania I had this great coach named Kathy. She was so tough, we called her Sarge. Some of the little kids were even afraid of her. But I just clicked with her. I worked with her for a long time, and by the time I left Silver Blades, I felt like I knew what she was going to say before she said it."

"So?"

"So, well—I miss her," Jill said. "I know Holly's a really great coach and everything—"

"She's the best," Sarah cut in. "And I was her favorite skater. I've worked with her for five years, even longer than you and Kathy. Then you come along and Ludmila and Simon are suddenly saying what a great skater you are, and Holly's so excited to be coaching you. And I'm told that I have to work with Matt. The coaches were so excited by you—nobody cared about what I wanted."

"But Ludmila told me—"

"Ludmila?" Sarah cried, her voice rising. "Did you talk about this with Ludmila? What are you trying to do, ruin my whole skating career?"

"No, of course not!" Jill protested.

"I wish you'd never come here," Sarah said, standing. "I wish you'd just stayed in Pennsylvania with your stupid coach, Kathy! Why don't you leave me alone?"

Sarah hurried out of the dining room, leaving Jill to stare at her half-finished lunch.

Good going, Jill, she said to herself. Now she hates you more than ever.

But Bronya is a real friend, Jill reminded herself. And there are a lot of other skaters at the school. Jill was sure she could be friends with some of them, such as Bridget or Meredith, if only she knew how. And something Ludmila had said had given her a great idea. She tried to put Sarah out of her mind and headed for the ice arena.

"Video," she said to herself. "That is the answer!"

Jill left the ice arena later that afternoon with a videotape in her hand.

"Jill! Jill! Wait up!"

Kevin was coming out of the rink, running toward her. She wasn't sure she was ready to talk to him yet. She hadn't spoken to him since they both got into trouble, and she hadn't forgiven him for lying to her about asking for permission to go to Denver. But she did kind of miss hanging out with him.

"Hey, I was watching the end of your practice today," Kevin said when he caught up to her. "You looked great."

"Thanks." Jill shrugged, and they started walking toward the dorms together.

"Listen, I'm really sorry I got you in trouble," Kevin said. "I didn't think things would turn out that way. I mean, maybe I did, but I shouldn't have included you. It really wasn't fair."

"Well, I guess I could have checked before I went off with you too," Jill said. "But don't ever lie to me again—okay?"

Kevin nodded. "Deal," he agreed. "And I'm *really* sorry that I haven't been hanging out with you for the past week. Talk about boring." He snored.

Jill laughed as they approached the Aspen House. "So do you think you're going to stick around?"

"Yeah." Kevin nodded. "I think so. Simon had a big talk with me about my chances to make the Nationals next year. I guess he thinks I can really do it if I want to. So I guess I'll hang out at the Academy awhile longer, see what happens. It could be worse."

"Yeah. I kind of made the same decision," Jill said. "But maybe we can do something to make this place more fun while we're here. I'm going to ask Lisa if I can have a small party this weekend. Don't worry— I'll get permission from *everyone* first."

"That's a great idea," Kevin said. Then he nodded at the videotape in her hand. "What's that?" he asked. "Another bad horror movie?"

"In a way," Jill said. "You'll find out soon enough."

13

"What's all this?" Kevin stood in the doorway of the Aspen House lounge, looking around at all the streamers hanging from the ceiling.

"It's video night," Jill said, placing a plate of cookies on the coffee table.

"No. Not another video review," Kevin said, sinking onto the couch beside Bronya.

Bronya shook her head. "Not like that."

"Then what is it?" Kevin asked, taking a cookie. "Oh—I get it—the mysterious tape! What's on it?"

"You'll see," Jill told him. She waited until the lounge filled up with other people. She'd invited everyone from school—except the coaches. Lisa was there to chaperone, but that was it.

"How did you pay for all this stuff?" Bridget asked, coming over to where Jill stood, by the VCR.

"I didn't," Jill said. "Not exactly. Lisa told me that

111

there's an entertainment fund set aside for students here, only no one's ever used it much."

"Really? I didn't know that," Bridget said.

"Yeah. We can use it for all kinds of stuff, like going to museums together, parties, whatever," Jill explained.

"Excuse me, Jill," Lisa said. "You have a telephone call."

"Oh, thanks," said Jill. She ran upstairs to the hall phone and said, "Hello?"

"Jill! We actually got you!" Tori cried.

"It's me," Jill said. "Live and in person. Where are you?"

"At my house again," Tori said.

"Hi, Jill," Danielle said. "I'm in Tori's kitchen."

"And I'm in her room," Nikki said. "I've never seen so many phones in one house before."

"So how's everything going?" Danielle asked.

"A lot better," said Jill. "How was the meeting about the spring show?"

"It was great," Tori said. "Everyone loved your idea for the theme—especially Mr. Weiler."

"And Nikki and Alex have the duet. They're going to skate a Romeo and Juliet routine," Danielle said.

Jill laughed. "Nikki, are you ready for that?" She could just imagine shy Nikki blushing throughout the entire program.

"I still can't believe it," Nikki said. "Having to pretend to be all romantic with Alex. He's just a *friend*—

nothing else. I'd rather not have the duet, thank you very much."

"But you guys must be getting pretty good, if they want you to do the duet," Jill told her.

"They are," Danielle chimed in.

"You've got to send me a picture of the two of you from the show so that I can put it in my scrapbook," Jill said. "I look at it all the time. I miss you guys a lot. But I'm actually starting to like it here."

"Good," Tori said. "Because we're already planning to visit you this summer. We've almost talked my mom into driving out. She wants to look at the school anyway."

"That sounds great," Jill said, smiling. "So, Nikki, what exactly do you have to do with Alex? Do you have to kiss him at the end?"

"Don't even say that!" Nikki cried. "And whatever you do, don't give us any more ideas—I'm in enough trouble now."

"You never know. I mean, this could be the beginning of something between you guys," Jill teased.

"Nothing is happening between me and Alex except skating. He's just my skating partner, not my boyfriend," Nikki said, and everyone laughed.

"What's all that noise in your dorm?" Tori asked. "It sounds like you're having a party."

"Actually I am," Jill said. "I'd better get back. I promised everybody a surprise, and they're all waiting for it."

"What kind of surprise?" asked Nikki.

"I'll tell you guys all about it—later," said Jill. "First I want to make sure it goes over okay."

"I can't wait to hear about it," said Danielle. "Good luck!"

"Thanks," Jill said. "And good luck with the spring show! I'll talk to you soon."

Jill hung up and hurried back downstairs.

"You'd better get started," Lisa whispered. "The crowd's getting restless."

"All right." Jill clapped her hands together. "Attention, everyone!"

"This isn't a class, is it?" one boy complained.

Jill shook her head. "No, trust me. Lights, please!" Bronya turned out the lights, and Jill turned on the tape in the VCR. "I rented that new skating movie, in case you guys want to watch it. But before that I have a very special tape."

After her meeting with Ludmila, Jill had borrowed the videotaping equipment from Matt, a coach, and made a tape of her own. Suddenly Ludmila's face appeared on the screen, in closeup. "You don't understand what I'm saying," she said. "Like this." In her ski parka she skated in a wide arc.

Jill paused the tape. "See her arms here? All wrong." She heard Bronya giggle. "And the footwork? Please!" She moved the tape forward. Simon was up next— she'd caught a perfect shot of him falling onto his backside while demonstrating a double flip to a young skater. "Terrible technique," Jill said as everyone laughed. "Just terrible."

The rest of the Skating Bloopers tape showed different skaters from the Academy trying jumps, spins, and just goofing around. Laughter filled the room. Ten minutes later, when the tape was over, everyone started clapping and cheering.

"They should send that to prospective students!" Jeff, Kevin's roommate, said.

"The International Ice Academy . . . the real story can now be told," Kevin said in a deep voice. "Film at eleven."

"That was great," Bridget said. "You should make one every week!"

"Maybe I will," said Jill. "Now, help yourselves to some snacks. I baked the cookies myself, so no bad reviews of those, okay?"

Jill put on some music, and people started dancing. She was replacing the pitcher of lemonade with a fresh one when Marie and Sarah walked over to her. Uh-oh, she thought. What now?

"That was a great idea," Sarah said to Jill. "The video, I mean. It was hilarious."

Jill stared at her in surprise. Sarah was actually saying something nice to her?

"I'm sorry about what I said to you the other day," Sarah said. "About wishing you'd never come and all that. I'm glad you're here."

"Thanks," Jill said softly.

"Sarah landed her triple toe loop today," Marie said. "Congratulations!" said Jill. "That's fantastic."

Sarah smiled. "Well, I realized that I might not have landed it if I hadn't switched coaches. I'd been working on it with Holly for ages, but it seemed like I was stuck in a rut." She paused and added, "I guess I was just frustrated, and I took it all out on you. You were really nice to try to talk to me today, after all the stuff Marie and I have done to you."

"I guess we should forget everything that has happened between us and start again," Jill said tentatively.

Sarah and Marie nodded in agreement, and Jill smiled.

"Great party," Marie said. "Everybody's having fun."

"Even Lisa." Sarah pointed to Lisa, who was dancing around the room with Kevin.

"I hope she doesn't tell Ludmila and Simon that I did a review of them," Jill said.

Sarah shook her head. "She won't. She's cool about stuff like that."

"Good," Jill said. "I thought she was."

Suddenly the music changed from a rock song to a hip-hop tune. Sarah grabbed Marie's sleeve and said, "Oh, I love this song. Come on!" She turned to Jill and added, "You can play your tapes whenever you want. Believe it or not, I love hip-hop!" Then she and Marie went off to dance.

Kevin walked up to Jill and wiped his forehead. "It's

turning into a sauna in here. I thought Lisa was never going to let me stop dancing with her."

"You're a good dancer," Jill said.

"Well, of course," Kevin said. "What did you expect?"

"No modesty, that's for sure. Hey, I want to get a picture of you and Bronya," Jill said. "Why don't you stand over there by the stairs. Bronya, come here for a second."

Bronya and Kevin stood by the stairs, Kevin towering over her by a full foot. To their right, there were kids dancing to one of Jill's hip-hop party tapes. To their left, people were talking and eating. "Okay, ready?" Jill asked, pointing her camera at them.

"Ready," Bronya said.

"Cheese," Kevin said. "Or should we say salchow?"

Just as Jill snapped the picture, Kevin wrapped his arm around Bronya's shoulders and squeezed. She shrieked with embarrassment, and the shutter clicked.

"You know what? This is going to be great in my skating scrapbook," Jill said, smiling at them.

"Imagine, Bronya—we'll be immortalized in Jill's famous scrapbook," Kevin joked.

"Come on, Bronya. Ignore him and let's dance," said Jill.

"Wait a second," Kevin said, following them into the group of people dancing. "Wait for me!"

Jill laughed as Kevin spun around in a circle to get past Marie and Sarah and nearly crashed into them. I should have had a party a long time ago, she realized. Everyone's having a blast—especially me.

Suddenly Jill couldn't wait for practice tomorrow morning, to get back out on the ice and do what she loved most in the world—skate. She had a feeling that after tonight she'd feel much more relaxed on the rink at the Academy too.

Another song came on, and Bronya and Kevin each grabbed one of Jill's hands. Look out, senior Nationals, she thought as her friends pulled her into the center of the room. Here comes Jill Wong!